The Little Light

Dipa Sanatani

The Little Light by Dipa Sanatani

Published by Mith Books, Singapore

www.dipasanatani.com

dipa.sanatani@gmail.com

E-book ISBN: 978-981-14-1679-8

In loving memory of Ratilal Mancharram

PRAISE FOR THE LITTLE LIGHT

No one I know of is writing like this today, and no book in recent memory has inspired so much envy in me. It has novelty and nuance from its first to its final paragraphs. *- The Bookish Elf*

The book takes us on a mythological and spiritual journey through time and space. The novel explores a sense of emotions that a human being feels in their lifetime. It is a novel of stages from life, death, beyond and all experiences in the middle. *- Delhi Wire*

This was a beautifully written, insightful, wonderful and entertaining read, which shouldn't be missed by anyone. A must read! *- Halo of Books*

This book got me hooked on the first page — a story derived from lore, spinning to this vibrant, magical story, that gives meaningful and memorable words of wisdom. I lost count actually of all the unforgettable quotes in there. *- Bookabilly*

One of the strengths of the novel is Sanatani's writing. She manages to bring human qualities to supernatural characters without compromising their wisdom or transcendent nature. With succinct narration and descriptive dialogue, Sanatani captures the unique characteristics of each Celestial Being — from the impulsive to the annoying to the level-headed. - *Parakeet Reviews*

This is perhaps the most delightful book I have ever read. It is not a novel, but... Fairy tale? Allegory? Myth? The closest to it is the myths of the Greek gods, but Dipa's pantheon is free of the savagery. We are introduced to superior beings who enter one at a time, and meet Little Light, who is a person on the way to being born. Only, these god-figures are all too human, and carry on just like any extended family on earth... In a way, the entire book is a prologue, in that it ends at a birth, presaged to lead to great things. I am looking forward to reading the life of the prophesized great person. - *Dr Bob Rich: Author of From Depression to Contentment*

Any reader with an interest in the spiritual and the world of fairy tale allegories would very much enjoy following the adventure of *The Little Light*. Dipa Sanatani writes with clarity and beautiful word choices to bring a complex story to life with clean, simple moments of discovery and drama. The meetings the light has with other characters are bold and colorful, and the Planet Party scene is one which is sure to stick in the heads of many younger readers and spark their imaginations. The book also brings about interesting talking points regarding its spiritual philosophy, which would be a great discussion starter in schools or youth groups, making *The Little Light* an intriguing but also educational read. - ***Readers' Favorite***

Dipa Sanatani is an artist. Her devotion was more to structure, substantive plot and form. I recognize the savviness involved in writing a myth/fantasy work emulating the form of a work of antiquity. The very idea is genius and it pulled off a testament to author's abilities. That artful adherence to structure and form made this book a truly modern fantasy novel fulfilling the many requirements of good storytelling. -***Read With Mit***

Contents

Chapter 1:

Song for Someone

"Welcome back, Little Light," Dag says to the tiny candle-shaped orange flame cradled in the palm of his hand. The flame dances and twirls, growing bigger and smaller. It burns without a wick, without a visible source.

"Do we know each other?" the Little Light asks Dag quizzically.

"In a sense... I am the Father Guardian of the Lore. You may call me Dag. I have long awaited your arrival."

"Why am I here? In your palm?"

"Your desire, and the desire of the Great Light, are one and the same. It is now that your light can manifest in the world of matter."

Little Lights are born into the world because of desire. Only immense yearning can give birth to the Little Lights. The Little Light that Dag holds in his hand is not the only Little Light that exists in the world. There are millions, billions - countless Little Lights that are, that were, and that will be. And all of these Little Lights are connected to each other in ways that are unforeseeable to the Little Lights themselves.

"What brings me back here?" the Little Light asks.

"A great destiny," Dag says.

"I am just a Little Light. No different to all the other Little Lights out there."

"Your humility is admirable. But you know as well as I do that you are destined for greatness."

"Why me?"

"Because you have prepared lifetimes for this. And now your time has finally come."

The Father Guardian of the Lore shuts his eyes. He sees the circumstances that will bring the Little Light into the world of matter. The image seizes him as though it were happening in the present moment. After all, to the Father Guardian of the Lore, time is a multifaceted cyclical concept, not a linear manmade one that only flows in one direction.

A solitary tear involuntarily rolls down Dag's left cheek. Some souls are born to families who have long awaited their arrival on earth. Other souls are born to families who do not want them. Dag wishes that it were different, but this is the way it has been since the Lore came into existence.

But once desire is born, it will manifest to fulfil its mission.

"Why are you crying?" the Little Light asks.

"I am your father, after all," Dag says. "The father of all that lives. And like any good father, I do not wish you to experience the profound pain you are destined to experience. The fulfilment of the desire that brought you into existence contains more suffering than what most souls can withstand in many lifetimes."

"But will I fulfil my destiny?"

"In the world of physical matter," Dag says, "everything has its price... Do you understand?"

It is a futile question. One that Dag asks of every Little Light that passes through his palm. But some Little Lights have a yearning so strong, a desire so great, that it is capable of changing the collective consciousness for generations to come.

"I understand," the Little Light says.

Dag nods. Once desires are born, they do not go away until they are fulfilled. And yet their fulfilment does not bring the rewards that one desires. The paradoxical nature of desire.

"Very well, then, Little Light," Dag says. "Very well, then."

∞

"Havah," Dag whispers. "I need you."

A woman appears. Her face is young, but her hands are old. Three large streaks of white line her long dark hair. Dag transfers the Little Light to his right index finger before carefully placing it in Havah's palm.

Havah takes a deep breath and releases it gently. The Little Light grows bigger. A tiny wick appears between Havah's hand and the Little Light.

"It has been many millennia since I felt a desire this... powerful," Havah says.

"It shouldn't surprise you, wise one," Dag says. "You are old enough to know that a new age is coming."

Havah nods. Her eyes have seen so much in the endless cycle of birth and death. She has seen ages come and go, civilizations rise and fall; the annihilation of whole species, and the birth of new ones.

It is the way of life. The nature of existence. Everything that is born has its time, and then it must die.

"Who are you?" the Little Light asks.

"I am Havah, the Mother Guardian of the Lore."

There was once a time - an age long ago, before time existed - where brother and sister, husband and wife - were one and the same. Dag and Havah come from that time. They too were once Little Lights that emerged from the Great Light. And they too, will one day have to return.

"Does the world welcome this Little Light's arrival?" Dag asks Havah.

"All Little Lights are welcomed. Especially one as powerful as this one."

"Do not speak in riddles, Havah. You know what I ask."

Havah breathes in and out. The Little Light is still a desire, without a vessel or a physical realm with which to fulfil its mission. But that will change very soon.

"Why do you ask questions for which you already know the answer?" Havah says. "You know why I do not answer."

Dag nods, and does not press Havah further. After all, Dag and Havah are both as old as time itself. There is nothing they have not seen. No story they have not witnessed. No Lore that is unknown to them.

Each Little Light that chooses to manifest into the world of matter has a multitude of uncountable options to choose from. Poor. Rich. Tall. Short. Man. Woman. Country folk. City folk. There are so many Lore to choose from that it is a wonder how each Little Light chooses its soul mission. The consciousness that pervades all things works in the most mysterious, yet calculating of ways.

"How long will the child suffer?" Dag asks.

"Dag, we have existed for eons," Havah says, "and yet, you never cease to amaze me with your ridiculous questions. You know I do not have the answers."

"Havah, you still have not learnt that I enjoy teasing you today as much as I did when existence came into being."

"You are incorrigible."

"As are you."

Dag and Havah smile at each other and lock hands.

"We," Dag and Havah say, "the Father and Mother Guardians of the Lore, summon the Nine Celestial Beings. We invoke your presence to bring forth this Little Light into the world. It is the Great Light's will, so let it be."

∞

"Let the planet party begin," Havah says with an exasperated sigh.

"Again," Dag says, rolling his eyes.

"Do you think they've changed?"

"Hah... them lot? They are always changing and yet somehow always manage to stay the same."

"We've known them for eons and it never gets old."

"The dysfunctional cosmic family."

"Indeed...Will the Celestial Beings support this Little Light's soul mission?"

"As you and I both know, that depends on whether or not circumstances are in alignment. They are bound by the laws that govern them, and each other. As are we..."

"Where are we?" the Little Light asks, interrupting the conversation. "What is this place? It is the most beautiful place I've ever seen…"

Dag and Havah smile. They've been here and done this so many times that they forget it is a moment of absolute splendor and wonder for the Little Light.

A room without walls stretches out into a star-filled sky that spins, twinkles, and dances. The Great Darkness intertwines with the Great Light to create a stunning, vibrating display. A realm abundant in natural beauty, secrets, and wisdom.

"We are in the Cosmic Womb," Havah says. "A timeless world. A vortex of eternal time – where the past, present, and future flow in a continuous stream."

"What is time?" the Little Light asks.

"Time is a wheel. A cycle that brings life into existence. Each age of mankind, each life is bound to this wheel. Once the wheel comes full circle, another cycle of time begins."

"I thought the Universe has existed for billions of years…"

"The Universe has existed for billions of cycles," Dag says. "Time is not linear, Little Light. When you have existed as long as we have, you will grow to understand that."

"And how old are you?"

"Far older than you can imagine. My eyes have seen more than most can bear."

Dag shakes his head and closes his dark eyes in the hope that shutting his eyes will stop him from seeing all that he has seen. *Nothing can erase those memories.* Havah gently places a hand on his shoulder. Dag quickly reopens his eyes.

"Oh Havah…" Dag says smiling secretly. "Oh yes, a hand on the shoulder…that makes it all just so much better."

Havah scowls at Dag. She raises her hand and smacks him. Dag purses his lips to suppress the laughter that's threatening to rush out.

"And the Celestial Beings? Who are they?" the Little Light asks.

"They are the ones who create and maintain time in the Universe," Havah says.

"Have I met them before?"

"Yes… You have."

"How come I do not remember?"

"You will when you see them again."

"I wish I could forget them," Dag interjects.

Havah laughs and throws her head back. Dag and Havah are the only beings in the universe that know what it's like to deal with *them* time after time.

"What are they like?" the Little Light asks.

"It depends on the circumstances..." Havah says, raising an eyebrow. "Anyways, you will meet them soon enough. And they will watch over you the rest of your existence."

"Watch over me? How? Why?"

"You are never alone, Little Light," Dag says. "You may forget this once you have manifested in the world of matter. But know that you are never alone. We are all here to usher your arrival into the world of matter, and we will watch over you always."

"Always?"

"Yes, always," Dag and Havah say together.

"Why?" the Little Light asks. "Why do you need to watch over me?"

"So that you may fulfil your soul's mission," Havah says with a tinge of melancholy.

"My soul mission... What's a soul? What's a mission? Who am I? What am I?"

Dag and Havah laugh. The Little Light is already asking big questions. Many Little Lights take millennia before they grow aware of their existence.

"You are an old soul, Little Light," Havah says, smiling. "A wise soul."

"You still didn't tell me what my soul mission is," the Little Light says.

"I cannot tell you that," Havah says in the calm voice of a mother talking to an over-inquisitive child. "It is against the Lore. Besides, we do not know everything. You have your part to play as well."

"My part? What's a part? Why must I play it?"

Havah takes a deep breath in, shaking her head, "I cannot tell you that either, Little Light. It is against the Lore. But for now... look around you. Relish the moment. Isn't creation magnificent?"

"It is. This place is so... profoundly beautiful."

Dag smiles. It pleases him to see the Little Light so full of joy - so marveled by the beginnings of manifestation. He wonders if the Little Light will remember this place and this moment. So few do... There was an age when humanity could access this memory - but that age is long gone. Very few can access the Lore: the memories of their creation, the memories of all creation.

When humanity was young, there were no Guardians of the Lore. The Great Light communicated with mankind directly. But things have changed. Now the Lore needs to be guarded, lest it fall into the wrong hands.

Dag and Havah were once human, too. But that was before...

"What's this... in the middle?" the Little Light asks.

A round table made of pure gold sits in the center: a perfect circle that's divided into twelve parts. Old runes, lines, and symbols mark the table. The engravings on the table are minute, intricate, and precise. Only a trained eye can understand and decipher these symbols. Without this round golden table... the Universe would cease to exist.

The table unlocks the mysteries of time and the Universe. When humanity was in its infancy, the Great Light taught humans how to read time and its relationship to space. That was many time cycles ago, and since then, humanity has forgotten the Lore. Humans have created their own concepts of time and no longer need the Cosmos to do that - or so they have come to believe.

"This is the Cosmic Round Table," Havah says. "It represents the Wheel of Eternal Time. The round table is 360 degrees - divided into 12 parts of 30 degrees each - representing the 12 constellations and the 12 astrological houses.

"This wheel tells the tale of the cosmic evolution of time and the soul's journey in it. This round table has the ability to see what humanity calls 'the past', 'the present', and 'the future'. It represents all that is outside humanity's control - the twin forces of fate and destiny. As the Mother Guardian of the Lore, this wheel is my responsibility."

"What about free will?" the Little Light asks.

"That is my domain," Dag says. "Think of me as a travelling tradesman. I barter what mankind freely gives up of its own volition. I work with free will to create new possibilities. I manipulate probabilities and create coincidences. But in the end, it is as it was written."

"It is as it was written," the Little Light repeats. "But if free will exists, then how can it all be as it was written?"

"In the Universe," Dag says, "every crossroads is predetermined. The choice is not. I know the tale that will come to pass with each choice, but I do not know which choice will be made."

"When I really think about it," the Little Light says, "life is a very strange experience."

"Indeed, Little Light, indeed," Dag says as he drifts off in his thoughts.

The memories of all that has been, all that is, and all that will be takes over his mind. The world is a mad and beautiful place. A beautiful and mad place, indeed.

Chapter 2:

Carry on my Wayward Son

Dag's meandering thoughts are interrupted by the sound of metal heels striking cold glass. Clink. Clink. Clink. Ah, yes...the first arrival. The Ascendant. The Lagna Lord.

"Did you hear that?" Dag asks.

"He's here," Havah says. "Our very first one. Walking backwards. Again. When he's not a speck on the surface of the Sun... he's in retrograde."

"My old friend Mercury," Dag says.

"You have strange friends..." Havah says disapprovingly.

"And even stranger partners..." Dag says under his breath.

"What did you say?"

"Err... Just what we need...Another Mercury in Retrograde baby."

☿

"Greetings," Mercury says as he takes his seat at the table. "Where is everybody? Ah... I see. I am the first to arrive at this planet party. How wonderful. I am the Lagna Lord: the Lord of the Birth Wheel."

Planet Mercury is in one of his two original forms. Original forms are the physical appearance a planet takes on when it is untouched by the cycle of time. Some planets have many original forms, others have only one.

Mercury's dark hair is neatly gelled. He's wearing a spotless white shirt and perfectly tailored black pants with pointy well-polished shoes. His smile is flawless and big, albeit a bit fake. When he expresses himself through masculine energy, he looks like a young businessman. When he expresses through feminine energy, he looks like a medicine woman. Mercury's domains are the mind, the intellect, and worldly intelligence.

He governs the constellations of Gemini and Virgo - the outer manifestation of the rational, practical, conscious mind.

"Welcome back, Great Wanderer," Havah says. "How's business?"

"Not a great time to sign contracts..."

Havah and Dag laugh. Mercury smiles and gives a snigger. There is an old superstition that Mercury in retrograde bodes a bad time for business. Many time cycles ago, humans used to believe that these periods were not a good time to start a new venture or make any irreversible decisions.

It's never a bad time for business, Mercury thinks. In the business world, there are always bad times and good times. What's important is to be prepared for both. Besides, people born when Mercury is in retrograde are the most innovative of thinkers.

"Oh, Mother Guardian," Mercury says as he takes off his pointy black shoes. "It's good to be home."

"I am pleased to see you."

"And I, you. Have you seen my Father lately?"

"Sorry to interrupt the catch-up," Dag says clearing his throat, "but we have work to do."

"A businessman never rests," Mercury says. "Good thing I'm so close to the Sun."

"You seem familiar," the Little Light says. "You're Budh."

Mercury offers a gentle smile that reaches his eyes. "I am known by many names, Little Light."

"I remember you. We've met before... You've changed your clothes."

"A businessman must keep up with the modern trends of fashion if he is to make a good first impression."

"I think you look ridiculous."

Mercury raises an eyebrow for a second before he throws his head back and laughs. Dag and Havah share a knowing expression. Mercury is used to making others laugh, but it's not often that someone makes him laugh.

"I like you, Little Light," Mercury says.

"I'm not sure I like you."

Mercury laughs again. Dag and Havah smile. Mercury reaches his hand out tenderly towards the Little Light. Havah gently passes the small flame burning on the wick to Mercury. The warm glow of the flame dances tenderly in his palm. Mercury shuts his eyes and takes a deep breath. Moments pass...

For so long, I have waited and yearned for the moment that I will finally get to see my star shining in the sky, illuminating brightly for all the world to see. This is not my first life. I have lived many lifetimes already, and only the Great Light knows whether it will be my last.

I have spent many lifetimes supporting the goals of others. Standing on the sidelines, nurturing their dreams. Some of them did great things with the support and care I provided. Others walked away with my precious gifts and squandered them.

For so long, I wondered when my day would come. And now, it is finally here. The Great Light has finally given me a great destiny. And, like every Little Light that is born into the world of matter, I will play my part in the Lore. My Lore is but one of the many Lore that have existed since the dawn of time.

But, unlike the Lore I have lived out before, this Lore is special. Because this Lore is mine and mine alone.

I am Little Light and the whole world will know my stories.

Mercury clutches his chest in awe, vividly feeling the Little Light's energy as though it were his own. Mercury slowly opens his eyes. His arms tremble at the sheer power and conviction of the Little Light's soul mission.

"Ahh... I see," Mercury says as he regains his composure. "I have not felt a desire this strong since..."

"We know," Havah says. "Best you say no more for now."

"Why won't you tell me?" the Little Light asks.

"All in good time," Dag says.

"I thought you said we're in the Cosmic Womb: the vortex before time comes into existence. So why must I wait?"

Mercury throws his head back and laughs again. "Little Light has a point."

"Rules are rules," Dag and Havah say in unison.

Mercury shrugs. No Celestial Being would dare to argue with the Guardians of the Lore. Their word is final. It is the Lore.

"Celestial Beings should not play favorites," Mercury says. "But I like you, Little Light."

"Am I supposed to like you back?" Little Light asks.

Havah smiles. Blessed by Mercury already. The quicksilver tongue that always has a comeback. Mercury shakes his head and grins.

"And in which point in the ecliptic do you intersect the eastern horizon?" Havah asks Mercury.

"The constellation of Gemini."

"One of your own constellations."

"Obviously. I am the first one here."

Havah rolls her eyes before grinning at Mercury and the Little Light. People born under Gemini Rising often appear younger than their age. Quick-witted and blessed with the ability to always see another's point of view - they are well-liked by many. Few can resist their humor, their charms, and their naughty way of getting what they want. But getting to truly know a Gemini's heart can be a challenge. Even to themselves.

"Have you seen the family?" Dag says.

"I have... But as the Lagna Lord, you know as well as I do that I only met them briefly. It's a political-business family. One with a long, powerful... and messy legacy."

"What?" Havah says, alarmed. "How could it be?"

"Why?" Mercury says, perturbed. "What's wrong with being born into a business family? This is the best age for it. Everyone wants to be born into one."

"The world of commerce is not this Little Light's destiny."

"Ahh, I see..." Mercury says as he stops for a contemplative moment.

There are only three reasons why a soul would manifest into the world of matter: if there is a karmic debt, if there is a soul lesson, or if the soul was born for the evolution of collective human consciousness.

"How could this soul have chosen to be born into a business family?" Havah asks.

"It is a wise real-world choice," Mercury says. "Anyone who doesn't understand the business world cannot survive in this age. Anyways, you know as well as I do that it is not I who chooses the family - it is the Little Light and the Great Light."

"But..."

"It is not like you to get so personally involved in the family the Little Light is born into, Havah. Why are you so alarmed?"

Havah averts her gaze from Mercury. There is so much she wants to say. But this is not the time. Not yet.

"I will tell you when everyone else is here," Havah says. "In the meantime, do you know anything else?"

"I know no more than that," Mercury says. "As the Lagna Lord, I can only tell you so much. We must wait for the others."

Havah nods; placated, but not appeased.

"May I begin the process of manifestation?" Mercury asks Havah.

Havah hesitates, a moment of melancholy in her eyes. It's always hard for a mother to watch her little ones grow up. She's done this so many times, but it still hurts - to know she must send a Little Light out into the cold, hard world.

Dag rests his hand on Havah's shoulder. "It's time to let go, Havah."

"But…," Havah begins.

"My love," Dag says in a firm, yet kind manner. "You must let go."

Havah takes a deep breath, nodding gently.

"You may begin," Havah says.

☿

The Lagna, or the ascendant, is the Little Light's very first moment of contact with its new life on earth. In a way, it is the beginning and the end; the Little Light's continuation from its last incarnation to its present one.

Whilst the Little Light itself is capable of holding all memories from its numerous lives, the physical manifested reality on planet earth comes with its own laws, structures, and boundaries. The physical body is the vessel with which the Little Light will attempt to complete its soul task.

As the Lagna Lord, Mercury is in charge of the physical appearance of the Little Light. The gender of the Little Light is still unknown, but Mercury begins molding a celestial body based on the family genetics. Mercury has briefly met all the ancestors and can pick and choose the physical traits and characteristics of the Little Light.

Not too tall, like the father's family, but not too short like the mother's family. Large feet and hands. Slender long arms and legs. Quick, almond-shaped eyes with a mischievous glimmer. A resilient body - one that heals swiftly from illness. A strong and well-proportioned skeleton. A sharp tongue and a curious mind - one that learns quickly, enjoys chatting and is able to charm any human with its knowledge and humor.

Mercury wants to do more, but he'll have to wait till everyone else gets here. For better or for worse, the Celestial Beings have to work together to make manifestation happen.

Mercury looks closely at the Little Light and smiles. There's something special about being a Little Light's ascendant. You are its first contact with the world of matter, setting the tone for everything that is to come.

"I," Mercury says, "the ruler of Gemini and Virgo, bestow upon you my gifts. It is the Great Light's will, so let it be."

Chapter 3:

The House of the Rising Sun

The Little Light grows into the fiery silhouette of an adult body that is 29.5 years old. The body is still androgynous - neither male nor female – but that will change soon enough.

"Wow," the Little Light says, looking at itself. "Thanks Mercury."

"You're welcome."

"So, how long will it take before I—"

"I know, I know," Mercury says, "I wanted to do more but we'll have to wait till…"

Mercury is interrupted by the sound of metal heels striking cold glass. Boom. Boom Boom. Ah, yes…the second arrival.

"I wonder who that is," Dag says.

"He's here," Havah says.

"Who?" Mercury asks.

"Daddy dearest," Havah answers.

"My old friend, the Sun," Dag says.

"You have strange friends…," Mercury says.

"What did you say?"

"Nothing…"

☉

"Welcome back to the Planet Party," Dag says as the Sun shows up.

"I am not a planet," the Sun says. "I am a luminary. It is I that sustains life on Planet Earth. I am the Earth's superstar."

"Hello to you, too," Havah says shaking her head. *I have no idea how Dag puts up with him – or even considers him a friend.*

"Not this again," Mercury says with a hand on his head. "It is exactly that kind of attitude that makes all the other planets despise you."

"They do not hate me. They are just jealous of me."

Mercury rolls his eyes. *Of all the people to be neighbors with, I am stuck with this luminous pain in the neck. And we almost always have to work together - arrogant, pompous, self-important, annoying… egomaniac. When will I get to run my own show?*

"There there, Mercury," Havah says. "You know I can read thoughts."

Mercury shrugs. His thoughts about his father shouldn't surprise anyone. No son wants to spend the rest of his life in his father's shadow. It is the way of the world, for children to outgrow their parents and find their own path.

The Sun has shoulder-length blond hair. A pair of dark sunglasses shields his eyes. Few have dared to look directly into his gaze and those who have, have not lived to tell the tale. His skin shimmers and glows like pure gold on a hot day. He emanates and holds more energy than most Celestial Beings can bear. It's hard, being center of the Universe, to burn day in and day out for everyone around you.

The Sun wears a huge gold watch on his wrist. The watch has a symbol of the Sun in the center with the other planets orbiting around it. He can see where and what the other Celestial Beings are doing at any given moment. The Sun is the only Celestial Being with that privilege. He wears a gold ring on every finger and bright yellow loafers. Even in his human-like form, he is difficult to look at, and yet it's hard not to look at him. You know you shouldn't stare, but you can't help it.

In a way, the Sun has the hardest life. Everyone needs him for their existence, but very few can handle him up close. Mercury, Venus, and the Moon are the exceptions - but it's tough, even for them. The Sun has a way of burning those closest and dearest to him.

"So, tell us," Dag says. "We're all waiting to know."

The Sun flashes his perfect white teeth in a beaming smile. Since the beginning of time, the Sun has represented the soul's Lore - the way the soul connects to the Great Light. With the passing of time, a lot of things can change, but no matter what happens, the soul's connection to the Great Light is something the Little Light can always come back to. That's why the Sun needs to burn as brightly as it does. Its light needs to illuminate the darkest corners of life's experiences.

"Are we in conjunction?" Mercury asks the Sun. *Please don't let us be in conjunction. Please don't let us be in conjunction.*

Mercury and the Sun usually end up sitting next to each other on the birth wheel. Mercury is never pleased about this - he'd rather have his own house, but in the cosmic dance of time, everyone has their part to play. And for Mercury that has almost always meant being overshadowed by light emanated by the Sun. We all have our destiny in this universe, even the Celestial Beings.

"I know you don't like being in the same house as me," the Sun says to Mercury with a tinge of melancholy. "But we are kin after all. I am your father..."

Here we go. The moment the Sun says the word 'father', Mercury stops listening. He puts on a mischievous smile and nods politely, saying 'umm hmm' now and then to give the impression that he's paying attention. *No way I'm listening to that spiel again. Enough with the guilt trip. I gave you life, provided for you, blah blah blah.*

Mercury sighs and unbuttons the top button of his perfectly pressed shirt. The ancient ones used to call Mercury 'the Messenger of God', for it was the son's duty to obey his father and do as he is told. As a child, Mercury didn't mind. He was in awe of his father's light, of his father's grace, of his father's generosity. But times have changed. Too many time cycles have passed. Mercury is not as young as he once was, but his father still refuses to let go of the grip he has on him.

The best Mercury can hope for is some time apart. Other than that, he is still stuck sharing the same house as his father. He wants to move out, but he can't. Mercury knows that the Sun prefers him when he embodies the constellation of Virgo - a young woman that personifies Daddy's Perfect Little Girl. The eternal maiden who never marries and is in awe of her father.

"Are you listening to me?" the Sun asks in an authoritative voice.

"No," Mercury says as he flashes another big cheeky smile.

"How dare you?" the Sun says. "I am your..."

"Father, yes I know. You keep reminding me. We are kin. Blah blah blah. Anyways, we all know you love the sound of your own voice, so what does it matter whether I'm listening or not?

"You talk, I nod, end of business."

Dag laughs, claps his hands, and smacks his knees. *As above, so below.* The great dysfunctional cosmic family. A deep hearty laugh reverberates through the Cosmic Womb. Havah smiles. She loves seeing Dag laugh; he does it so little these days. He really is getting too old and too tired for the never-ending cycle of life and death.

"Oh, Mercury," Dag says. "You children really do have a way of seeing the heart of the matter."

"Why, thank you, Dag," Mercury says, grinning.

"How dare you take his side," the Sun says, indignant. "I thought we were friends. You owe me your loyalty, Dag."

Dag's smile fades. He stares at the Sun, his eyes resolute and firm. "Old friend, it would be unwise to take that tone with me. Unlike the rest, I need neither you, nor your light to survive. Show some humility."

The Sun opens his mouth to say something, but he stops himself. He's known for some time now that the other Celestial Beings find him too proud. But it's not his fault that he shines so brightly. That he's so beautiful. So amazing, so awesome. The Superstar of the Celestial Beings. The one that rules over each day and the solar year. The one and only Sun. The Light of the Universe, the Earth, the World, the—

"What's the Little Light's sun sign?" Mercury asks the Sun to ease the tension in the room. The sun sign represents the solar month that a soul chooses to manifest in the world.

"Pisces," the Sun says.

"Pisces?" Havah repeats with a surprised twinkle in her eye. "Perfect. Just perfect. Exactly what we need..."

"Perfect?" Mercury barks. "You've got to be kidding me. What is this? Some kind of cosmic joke? You know how much I hate being in Pisces. It's a cruel placement. You've blessed this Little Light with tremendous intelligence yet damned it to think with its heart. Feelings cloud the intellect! How many times do I have to tell you people? I can be in just about any sign, but Pisces? WHY PISCES? I DON'T WANT TO BE AN EMOTIONAL BASKETCASE!"

Dag, Havah, and the Sun stare at Mercury, stunned. For someone who claims to be ruled by intellect, Mercury's emotional outbursts are more irrational than any other Celestial Being's. The ancients believed that Mercury is debilitated in Pisces. The truth is, it's not a bad placement to be. It forces Mercury to deal with the black box of his emotions.

The Sun can be in any constellation and be content there for he shines so brightly that he can burn the bad and illuminate the good. But for Mercury, it's different. He hates being in Pisces. He can gift people with intelligence, aptitude in business, and medicine - but allowing people to think with their heart? It's the equivalent of asking a businessman to write poetry.

Why would the Great Light do that to anyone? It's bad for business and the poetry is terrible.

"Mercury," Havah says.

"Reading my thoughts again?" Mercury asks, his tone brisk. *Bloody Mercury in Pisces. I don't belong there. Just keep me away from those water signs...*

"I know you don't like it," Havah says. "But it is for the best. There are other things at stake here."

"Why did the Great Light bless this Little Light with intelligence if it is not to use it? Sometimes I feel like the Great Light is a puppet master and we are all its puppets..."

"As you said," Havah says, "one cannot survive in this age without knowledge of the business world."

"You cannot do this to me."

"You have no choice," Havah says.

"Be quiet, everybody," Dag says.

His voice is low yet strong. Like most men who have aged gracefully, Dag knows that true power is in restraint, not in lashing out.

"Mercury," Dag says. "The Great Light has chosen to manifest compassionate intelligence through you. Treat it as an opportunity to learn about another layer of consciousness. I know you rule over the intellect, but remember that the world of emotions, of spirit, and of compassion is far older. The Universe can exist without intelligence. It cannot exist without compassion. It will do you well to remember that."

"Compassion? After all that we have seen, and all the ages that have gone by, how can you possibly believe that? It defies all logic."

"Looks like it isn't just the Sun that needs to keep its ego in check. The world may well love the fruits of business and medicine, but the world can live without you, Mercury. It cannot live without the Sun. It will do you well to remember that."

Mercury is about to open his mouth, but he decides to remain quiet. Arguing with Dag is always futile.

⊙

"You must be Surya," the Little Light chimes in.

"Like Mercury here, I have many names," the Sun says.

The Sun's expression softens. He's always happy to meet a Little Light. The other planets - even his son, Mercury - may not like him, but to all the Little Lights, he brings hope; something that they can always come home to. The Sun symbolizes the soul, the essence, and all that is good about life.

The dawn. The summer harvests. The summer festivals. The bright light at the end of the dark long tunnel. For eons, mankind even worshipped the Sun, built temples in his name, held great sacrifices and hearth fires at the solstices. That era has passed, but still humans acknowledge the Sun as the source of all life on earth. Without the Sun, life as we know it would cease to exist.

Unfortunately, no one ever stops to think about how hard it is to be the Father of the Universe. The breadwinner of the cosmos. The lonely provider that must give and give and give.

"Mercury blessed me with his gifts," the Little Light says.

"My son has done well," the Sun says. "Your astral body is beautiful."

"Stop calling me, 'my son'," Mercury says haughtily. "I have a name, you know."

"Must you always talk back?"

"Must you always treat me like an extension of you?"

"I am your father…"

Oh no, the F word again. Like clockwork, Mercury immediately stops listening. He mischievously puts on a smile and nods, politely saying 'umm hmm' now and then…

"Is he always this way?" the Little Light whispers in Mercury's ear.

"Believe it or not, he's mellowed," Mercury whispers back. "He used to be even worse. Thankfully, the humans stopped building temples for him. His ego was even bigger back then."

"What are you two talking about?" the Sun barks.

"Nothing important," Mercury says, quickly changing the topic. "Enough with our father-son squabbles. We must begin manifestation."

"Ah, of course," the Sun says. "My apologies, Little Light. Please give me your hand."

The Little Light stretches its silhouette-like hand towards the Sun. The Sun tenderly takes the Little Light's hand in his. The Sun is so large that the Little Light's adult astral body looks like a three-year old child next to his.

"Ah..." the Sun says, sensing the Little Light's soul mission. "Your light is far warmer and brighter than what I've seen in generations... In fact, since...."

"You know the rules," Havah says. "We will talk about it once everyone is here."

The Sun nods. "My apologies, Havah. You know how we all get carried away."

The Sun takes the Little Light's hand and places it on his heart. Unlike the other planets that have the ability to bless Little Lights with gifts and challenges, it's different for the Sun.

For the Little Light to manifest in the physical world, the Sun has to give a spark of himself to the Little Light so that his essence, and that of the Little Light, are one and the same. A part of the Sun will always shine inside the Little Light, come what may.

Life can be full of pain, suffering and strife, but this spark will always remain untouched because it belongs to the source of all life on earth. Nothing and no one can take it away because it is a gift from the father to all his children. It can never be tarnished or spoilt. It exists and will continue to burn bright till the death of the physical body.

Mercury, Dag and Havah quickly close their eyes and avert their gaze from the scene. No one - neither the planets nor the Guardians - are allowed to witness the splitting of the Sun. It is against the Lore. Those who disobey risk complete annihilation.

A bright orange solar ray bursts through the room. A spark from the Sun's heart detaches itself from the Sun's body. It lingers briefly in the Cosmic Womb before it makes a home in the Little Light's heart.

The Little Light's hair grows longer, crowning the head in a luscious display of lights before settling on a mane that resembles a lion's. The astral body grows smaller at the waist and rounder around the hips. A woman's body begins to take shape. She's dressed in a turquoise dress embroidered with two fishes swimming in opposite directions: a representation of the final constellation of Pisces. The Little Light's eyes take form - auburn with golden centers. It is the Sun that gives the gift of vision to humanity. It is with the eyes that we learn to see the world, and that the world sees into us.

The Sun falls to his knees, weakened and tired. He yells out in agony, clutching his chest. It hurts him every time he splits himself. He dies a little with each birth. But that is the Lore. Everything, no matter how great or how powerful, must one day pass. The Sun is no exception. He destroys himself to create the world.

"You're an incredibly beautiful woman," the Sun says, gazing at the Little Light with the eyes of a proud father.

"Thank you, Father," the Little Light says. "For breathing life into me."

"It is my duty."

The Little Light looks at her arms and touches her face with her hands. She has a high forehead with voluminous hair. A sharp nose and strong cheekbones. Small lips and a big smile. A regal face.

"What am I?" the Little Light asks.

"Maiden, mother, crone," the Sun says as he takes a good look at the Little Light. "May the world welcome my beloved daughter with open arms."

The Sun gets up and gives the Little Light a twirl. She giggles. He smiles.

Mercury turns around. His heart fills with nostalgia. The Sun was such an amazing father when he was a young boy. A part of him wishes that he could be that young boy again, the one that played on his father's knee. But no one, not even the Celestial Beings, can remain untouched by the cycles of time.

Mercury looks longingly at the Little Light. She is indeed beautiful - luminous, full of hope, full of laughter. Her light shines like no other Little Light he's ever seen. But something inside him feels unsettled.

"You look worried, Mercury," Havah whispers in his ear.

"She is the first born in a political-business family," Mercury says. "Sun in Pisces, Mercury in Pisces with a Pisces midheaven. The business world is no place for a soul like this."

"What are you worried about?"

"Unlike my father, I spend my days and nights watching people on earth. I don't have the luxury of being up in an ivory tower. The family is not a good match. Given this Little Light's destiny..."

"No soul - no matter how great or how small - can avoid pain. Sometimes the greater the destiny, the greater the amount of pain. Know that nothing lasts forever. That all things must come to pass. As above, so below. As the Lagna Lord, you have a lot to teach the Little Light, and she has a lot to teach you. The Celestial Beings must evolve with humanity, Mercury."

Mercury nods and smiles, the bad feeling in his stomach deepening with each passing moment.

⊙

"As the Father of your Universe," the Sun says to the Little Light, "I grant you one wish."

"A wish?"

"Yes. You may ask for anything you want."

The Little Light stops to think. Over the passage of time, the Sun has heard all kinds of requests and he has granted all of them. Unfortunately, sometimes you have to get your heart's desire to know that it's not your heart's desire.

"Anything?" the Little Light asks the Sun.

"Of course, my child," the Sun says. "Anything you like."

"May no night be too long. May no day be too bright. Shine on my life warmly and gently. Promise me you will rise each morning and set each day. My soul is old enough to know that I must accept life's dark days. But promise me that you will never allow the darkness to break my spirit. Promise me that you will never abandon me. Promise that you will always be there to light my path and guide my way."

The Sun smiles. It is a wise wish - not many Little Lights know what to ask for. Lifetimes go by in this manner before consciousness penetrates the soul and becomes one and the same.

"I promise," the Sun says. "It is indeed you, isn't it?"

"My time has come," the Little Light says.

The Sun's adult body morphs into that of a child. Small. Full of joy. Full of hope. Vulnerable, yet open and unafraid. Innocence at its purest - born of pure light.

"Pick me up," the Sun says.

The Little Light lifts the Sun and cradles it as a mother would a child.

"Who am I?" the Little Light asks. "Who are you?"

"You are me, and I am you," the Sun says. "Your light will exist as long as I do. You are Liora. The Chosen Light of the Great Light."

Chapter 4:

Bad Moon Rising

"**M**y love," a woman's voice calls out. "I have not seen you in this form in millennia."

The woman stands tall and proud. She wears a blue knee length tunic embroidered with gold stars. Her body is strong yet svelte. She wears brown sandals on her slightly calloused feet. A cape made of a wolf with yellow eyes rests on her back. Her hair is silver. On her forehead, she wears a headpiece of the full moon. Her skin is terribly cratered, but shimmers in a soft, beautiful, luminous perfection. Her black eyes are dark, deep and penetrating. Her lips are wine red. She carries a bow and an arrow.

The Sun immediately transforms himself back into his adult form. The last person he wants to see him as a child is her. She has not seen him in that way since...

"Why do you greet him before you greet me?" Mercury asks haughtily.

The woman laughs. Mercury is more like his father than he likes to admit. She's wondered for some time now if her son will one day understand what it means to be a man: to truly take on the responsibility that the Sun has. It takes such a long time for boys to grow up.

Women have the waxing and waning of the moon to guide them. Maiden. Mother. Crone. But men? They have no such dramatic transitions. No monthly bleed governed by the Moon. No menarche. No menopause. No dramatic bodily rites of passage.

Mercury used to be such a playful and curious child that did nothing but idolize and look up to his father. But as Mercury got older, he wondered, as many young men do, about the day he'll take over his father's shoes. But the Sun is a luminary, one that all the other Celestial Beings are bound to orbit around. Mercury will never have his own solar system, and someday he'll need to accept that. He is a scion - a highly prized scion - but one that is destined to be in the Sun's shadow for the rest of his days. The best he can hope for is a little breathing space now and then.

"Who are you?" the Little Light asks. "The other two I recognized... But you... I feel I know you, but..."

The woman smiles. Some Celestial Beings have two forms, others have only one. But she... she changes every two and a half days. She is the most mutable of all them. Like the Sun, she is also a luminary. There are many moons in this galaxy, but she is the closest luminary to earth. In the past, people revered her for who she truly is - the Sun's equal partner. But these days, humans call her a satellite, like those manmade objects they've been sending out in the sky to study the Cosmos.

"You called the Sun, 'my love'," the Little Light says. "Are you his wife?"

"I am no one's wife," the woman barks, momentarily offended.

The Sun grins. She's always a handful whenever she takes this form. But he loves her spunk. Her tenacity. The fact that she's independent and doesn't need him. It's when he wants her the most.

"She is the Warrior Moon," the Sun says. "She belongs to no one and no one belongs to her. She is Diana."

Unlike the Sun, which is too bright to even gaze at, mankind can gaze at the Moon directly. It is the Moon that guides humanity in those dark hours. It is the Moon that allows mankind to see the glory of the night sky's jewels. And it is the Moon that mankind first landed on, having defied the earth's gravity. The Moon is the Mother. Always there. Always watching. Sometimes she can even be seen during the day. Unlike the Sun who shines brightly and is forever out of reach, the Moon is close. She is the Earth's closest kin. Mankind's very first teacher.

"Moon in Aries," Havah says and laughs. "Greetings, sister."

The two women embrace. There is something similar about the two of them.

"You are Chandra," the Little Light says. "I have never seen you like this - so magnificent...so... proud... so brave. I always saw you as the nurturer."

"I am many things, Little Light. Unlike the Sun, I am forever changing."

"Why?"

"Because everything in life has its own Lore, its own purpose."

"And what is my Lore?"

"You will have to discover that for yourself. Now, please take my hand."

The Little Light puts her hand in Diana's. Their palms touch. Diana takes a deep breath. The Sun may well be the one that brings the new dawn, but it is the Moon that taught men to count the days and the months. To navigate life in those dark times. The Moon knows mankind more intimately than any other Celestial Being, and vice versa.

"An old soul," Diana says. "A very old soul."

"It is not just an old soul, Diana," the Sun says. "It is Liora."

Diana and the Sun stop to look at each other for a moment. A knowing glance of surprise and curiosity passes between the two of them.

"The Chosen Light of the Great Light..." Diana says. "There has not been one in... That means..."

"Not now, sister," Havah says, irritated. "We will talk more when the rest are here."

Diana nods and gently lays her right hand over her left hand, feeling Little Light's warmth.

"I have not felt a desire this great in a long time," Diana says. "Is that why you were in child form?"

The Sun nods. The Celestial Beings existed long before mankind, and yet their destinies remain inextricably linked. The Cosmos have gazed down on earth, and mankind has gazed up at the Cosmos. Would one exist without the other?

"Moon in Aries," the Little Light says. "What does that mean?"

"Good question, " Diana says. "I believe you have met my son, Mercury. He is the ascendant, the Lagna Lord. That first impression. Your ascendant is in Gemini."

"When people first meet you," Mercury chimes in, "they'll encounter many of my amazing qualities - funny, childlike, quick-thinking, intellectual, chatty, a fantastic communicator, intelligent, witty—"

"Mercury," Diana interrupts, "show some humility... Anyways, when people get to know you a little better, they'll encounter your Sun Sign."

"Which is in Pisces," the Sun says. "They'll see that you're creative, dreamy, highly intuitive, and spiritual."

"You have no idea how much I hate being in Pisces," Mercury says. "Bloody quackery with no basis in…science, logic, or any rational understanding…"

"You made your opinion perfectly clear earlier," the Sun says. "It would do you some good to appreciate the reality beyond what we can see and perceive. And just because you cannot perceive something, doesn't mean it doesn't exist."

"Dag already said that," Mercury says. "Do you always have to be so self-righteous in the way that you teach things? Do you have to burn away at every single one of my opinions and ideas?"

Diana clears her throat. "Gentlemen… Simmer down. This is Liora's Planet Party. Not yours."

"Liora…" the Little Light says. "The Sun called me that earlier, too. Is that my name?"

The three Celestial Beings look at each other uncomfortably. Most Little Lights are oblivious to whatever goes on at these Planet Parties. But this Little Light is different…

"Yes, that is your name," Dag says in a heavy voice. "And if these three Celestial Beings weren't so busy having the same old cosmic family drama, they'd do a better job of ushering you into the world of matter.

"Mercury, do us all a favor and stop arguing with your parents. You are the Lagna Lord and you will always rule over the way the Little Light communicates and expresses herself in the world. Pisces is the oldest zodiac sign. It has travelled through all the constellations. That is why it is as dreamy and disoriented as it is wise and intelligent.

"Mercury, remember that you are young. You are intelligent - none of us doubt that - but you are far younger than the Sun and the Moon, and therefore far less experienced. I know you want to prove yourself. And one day you *might* get the chance. But till then, stop being the obnoxious teenage kid who thinks he's all grown up and knows everything."

Mercury opens his mouth, to protest, but Dag raises his eyebrows and a finger. Mercury gives in and sits down.

"The ascendant is the mask," Dag tells the Little Light. "The face you put on when you greet the world. The Sun is your Self. Your ego. Your core. Your consciousness. It's your heart of hearts. The indestructible energy your soul chose to manifest in this world."

"And what's the Moon?" the Little Light says.

"I am your instinct," Diana says. "If the Sun is your consciousness, then I am your subconscious. I am the part of you that remains hidden from the world but is nevertheless running the show in a very real way. I am your mind. That first reaction. Only those closest and dearest to you will see this side of you."

"What does it mean?" the Little Light asks. "To have your Moon in Aries?"

Havah and Diana smile at each other.

"It means," Diana says, "that you are a warrior. A fighter. Fiercely independent. No holds barred. Take no prisoners. If anyone dares to mess with you they better watch out. You will bruise easily and heal quickly. But since this is your Moon sign, this strength will be silent. Hidden. A hidden fire will forever burn inside you like a silent volcano. This fire will wax and wane, but it can never be vanquished."

The Little Light momentarily closes her eyes. She can feel the quiet yet smoldering fire burning and pulsating inside her. When she opens her eyes, amber flames light them up.

"I like this," the Little Light says. "I feel brave, independent... and curious."

Diana smiles. Aries is a strong energy, but its fire is not like that of the Sun. The Sun is always burning, always shining, always giving, always expecting adulation. The Aries fire is independent and doesn't need anyone. It burns of its own accord.

"Of all the Moon Signs," Havah says, "Diana - the Moon in Aries - is the only one who never marries. She is the Goddess of the Hunt, capable of providing for herself even in the darkest hours of the night."

"My favorite Moon Sign," the Sun says, gazing at Diana, eyes filled with longing.

"Truth be told," Diana says, "men love a woman with Moon in Aries, but most of them can't handle it."

The Sun's admiring glance morphs into a glare. Even the sunglasses can't hide his irritation.

"Oh, how I enjoy teasing you," Diana says with a haughty grin.

The Sun's expression shifts to an exasperated sigh. His eyebrows relax and he smiles - a smile that an amused adult gives a charmingly naughty child. "And how I enjoy to be teased by you."

The two luminaries embrace, eyeing each other like two strangers meeting at a party, flirting with each other for the first time. The Sun runs his fingers through Diana's hair, gazing into her eyes longingly.

"Gross," Mercury barks. "Get a room. To think you called me a teenager... As you said, this is Liora's planet party, not yours."

Chapter 5:

Tears of the Dragon

"The brighter the light, the darker the shadow," an ominous voice whispers in a slow and deliberate manner. "If it isn't the two pompous, arrogant and condescending luminaries. Your son is right, you know. You really should get a room."

"Must that demon always gate-crash every planet party?" the Sun asks with disdain as he pulls away from Diana. "You do not belong here. You never did. Why don't you go back to the dark pit where you ordinarily dwell?"

"I am no demon, Surya," the voice says. "I am your shadow. You know as well as I do that I can only appear in the ecliptic whenever you embrace your beloved Chandra, Diana, Luna or whatever her name is on that given day. If the two of you cease to embrace, then I will also cease to be. But like clockwork, you embrace, and every time you do, I appear."

"Aren't you tired of being the only outsider at this planet party?" Diana says angrily. "We've never accepted you, and we never will."

"Good thing I have other friends," the voice says. "Not all other Celestial Beings feel the way you do. They know that without me, humanity would never wonder about the purpose behind its existence. You pompous luminaries will lose all your admiring fans: those stargazers who look up to the skies seeking answers to the questions that define their lives."

Diana stares at Ketu: the South Node of the Moon – the necessary dark night of the soul created so that humanity can attain enlightenment, peace and progress. Ketu forces the soul to be accountable for its past deeds, for in every action there is an equal and corresponding reaction. When we choose one road, we inevitably forsake its opposite – an uncharted course that must one day be walked upon, so the universe can regain the elusive balance that keeps it all together.

Ketu is the antithesis to every planet. Whilst all the other planets bestow gifts and challenges, Ketu does the very opposite; it takes away and plunges the soul deep into a never-ending pit of darkness till…

"C'mon boys and girls," Havah says in a gentle mocking voice. "Play nice."

The Sun and Diana purse their lips. This saga has gone on since humanity's creation, and it will continue to exist till humanity is ready to return to the Great Light.

"Hello, old friend," Mercury says with a rare genuine smile.

"Mercury," the voice says, softening slightly. "It's good to see you."

"I wish I could say the same. C'mon, don't hide in the shadows. Show yourself."

A loud hissing sound reverberates through the Cosmic Womb. The Sun and Diana show a momentary flicker of fear. They will never openly admit it, but they have been afraid of *it* since humanity's age began. Since they unwittingly created *it* and brought humanity into existence.

A towering bejeweled ethereal serpent appears. It is pure white and laced with uneven silver patches. Unlike the other Celestial Beings, which can take on a multitude of human and non-human forms, this being is different. It is a shadow, a reflection, a wave. The serpent shifts, sways, and dances, indulging those present in a marvelous spectacle of light and dark.

"Greetings, Ketu," Dag says. "Welcome back."

"Thank you, Dag," Ketu says.

♄

"Greetings Great White Serpent," the Little Light says. "I know you."

"Indeed, indeed," Ketu says. "All Little Lights know me. I am one half of the twin pillars of desire and destiny. Some fear me, whilst others find my presence oddly comforting. What do you feel, Liora?"

"I feel... No, not feel. I see... a great destiny. An important purpose for my existence."

"All Little Lights have a destiny and purpose, but yes... your soul's yearning is particularly strong. And... there is another soul like yours. A twin."

"A twin? Why? Isn't my light enough? I thought all souls were created equal and perfect. So why the twin?"

"Because polarities must come together, merge, create a third form, and then separate once more. This is how it has been since the beginning. Everything in the world of matter has its equal and opposite counterpart."

"Do you have an equal and opposite counterpart?"

"Of course. You will meet him soon enough. I cannot exist without him, nor him without me. We are a singular entity that was split into two so that we could reunite once more. Together, we can ascend to greater heights than we ever could alone."

"I see," the Little Light says.

The Little Light reaches out to touch Ketu, but her hand goes through the shifting serpent in front of her.

"You are not like the others," the Little Light says. "You cannot take on a physical form. You are surreal. A phantom. An illusion."

"Just because I am an illusion does not make me any less real, Little Light," Ketu says.

It is true that unlike the other planets, Ketu has no physical form. Its influence is far subtler, operating beyond mundane reality.

"If the Sun is the consciousness," Ketu says, "and Diana is your subconscious, then I am the superconscious. I am the invisible force behind humanity's destiny and its desire. I may not be made of matter, but I exist in every Little Light, and in the collective consciousness that ties all humanity to the Wheel of Time.

"I represent your karma – the past deeds of your soul and the lessons it has mastered. You see, Liora – life is a school where souls take on physical form to learn, grow, and expand the consciousness of each individual soul, and of humanity as a whole."

The Little Light takes a step towards Ketu and observes her carefully before taking three steps back. The Little Light becomes disoriented, confused, and heavy. An uneasy silence hangs in the Cosmic Womb.

This moment has never been easy.

"You have so many memories," the Little Light says, clutching her chest. "You carry unbearable burdens – of lives lived and of lives yet lived; of accomplishments and of the price paid to achieve them; of old victories and new yearnings. Despite your formless form, your presence feels heavy and lonely. You are clouded in nostalgia that feels real, even though it is long gone."

Ketu takes a deep breath and sighs in defeat. She sighs the same way that humans do when they know they have to accept things that they cannot change. Unlike the other Celestial Beings that can bestow gifts and challenges, Ketu is different. She is the custodian of each Little Light's past actions and deeds – of what has been done and cannot be undone. She remembers each experience and each decision; the countless memories of all births gone by are stored inside her. Ketu is the wavering personification of past accomplishments, trials, and tribulations that no Little Light can ever erase. Our deeds stay with us forever. We cannot forget them no matter how hard we try.

"Who was I?" the Little Light says in anger. "What did I do that was so wrong that I am to be reborn in a world of men? To be born is to know suffering. To know pain. To know fear. To know deep yearning that can never be satisfied."

Ketu sighs again in that weary sense of defeat. She is used to this rejection. No Little Light, however wise, wants to be separated from the Great Light. It is a moment of great anguish and deep pain – to remember all the soul's memories, only to lose them and be reborn into a world where it takes unbearable pain, suffering and darkness to bring forth the light once more. But that is humanity's destiny; to evolve and grow with the cycles of time.

"If the human experience is born of compassion," the Little Light says angrily, "why does the Great Light curse humanity to suffer in the most unspeakable of ways? Why is there so much grief, pain, and tragedy in the world?"

Ketu gives a sardonic smile. The questions are easy to answer, but difficult to fully comprehend. It is one thing to gain knowledge, and another to experience it and fully understand its true meaning.

Ketu snaps her fingers and morphs into a beautiful woman. She wears a white gown adorned with the finest crystals that radiate splendid light. Her silver hair flows down to her waist. She looks young, but there is something in her eyes that gives away her true age. A huge gem in the shape of a teardrop rests in the center of her forehead, a third eye that can see the past in the present moment.

"Life can only be lived forwards," Ketu says, "and truly understood backwards.

"Little Light, you have spent numerous past lives supporting others, infusing your power and your majesty into seeing your loved ones succeed. Now, your soul is given the chance to shine on its own, and not just for itself, but for all of humanity.

"You are born with a Ketu in Libra. For what you have sown in past lives, you will reap in this life. I know it must have been hard, watching those around you go forth and push ahead with the strength you gave them. I know that you did so willingly, with no expectation of gain or reward. But now the time has come, for you to know your true self and all that it is capable of achieving on its own.

"I know you see it, how your next incarnation will bring you grief, separation, and loss from your loved ones. But from these experiences, a new dawn is emerging. A new era is on the horizon.

"Your soul is tied to all other souls, and their souls are tied to yours in an inextricable way. Do not fear, Little Light. It is now your turn to seize your destiny. The world is waiting for you."

The Little Light moves further away from Ketu. There are too many memories. They rush forth like the ocean's waves – incoherent and tumultuous – all those old lives lived, crashing into each other drop by drop. This is why souls forget the details of their past lives when they are born. It is all too much.

"Take my hand," Ketu says. "You must remember before you can forget."

"No," the Little Light says. "I will not."

"Please, take my hand."

"I will do no such thing."

"I cannot force you to do what you do not desire, but know that you will take my hand of your own volition when the time comes. No soul can forsake its karma."

Dag walks towards the Little Light and lays a gentle hand on the silhouette's shoulder. No father willingly sends one of its children out into the world to suffer. But it is the way of the world. Life isn't easy, or even fair. "It is as it was written," Dag says. "It is as it was written."

ʊʊ

"You know what you need to do," Ketu says to Mercury.

Mercury nods, suddenly serious. As the Lagna Lord, the ascendant, it is only Mercury who has access to the external physical body that has been, and the physical body that will be. Mercury removes a small white urn from his jacket pocket. He collected it before arriving in the Cosmic Womb.

The urn contains the ashes of the body from the previous incarnation on earth. Not all humans are fortunate enough to get a cremation or burial - some die in war, others are murdered - their bodies, still undiscovered. Other bodies are left open for the elements in the cycle of life.

Many humans believe that the soul of the body continues to linger on earth if it is not given proper funeral rites. Perhaps there is some truth to that. Nevertheless, one thing is for certain; the physical body is worthless once the soul departs. It is the Lore.

"Is that me?" the Little Light asks, looking at the urn.

"In a sense, yes," Mercury says. "It is what's left of you. What's left of your last incarnation on earth."

"What are those markings?"

Mercury traces his fingers over the symbols on the urn. Some symbols are large, representing stronger energy patterns and soul ties, whilst other symbols are small, minute; representing the things that come and go with the passing of life's seasons.

"Only Ketu can tell you that," Mercury says.

"I do not wish to speak to her."

Ketu is about to say something when Mercury raises his hand to silence her. Ketu closes her mouth and retreats. Mercury opens the urn and empties its contents onto the Cosmic Round Table. A few handfuls of ash pour out onto the Wheel of Time.

"Wow..." the Little Light says. "All those years... All those memories... All dust."

"Not dust, Little Light," Mercury says. "This is ash."

"What's the difference?"

"Ash is the purest substance on earth. It is what is left when matter has been completely purified by fire."

"How can so much reduce to so little?"

"Nothing in this world is ever created or destroyed, it can only be transformed."

Mercury closes his eyes and takes a deep breath. It surprises him that the Great Light has entrusted him with the task of being the Lagna Lord for a soul as powerful as this one. Ever since he came into being, Mercury has been indulged and nagged like the baby of the family. He never thought that the Great Light would ever give him such a big responsibility.

"Mother," Mercury says, addressing Diana, "I need your blessing."

"Of course, my son," Diana says, "of course."

Diana removes a strand of her hair and curls it into a ball. She clasps it in between her hands and slowly begins to let go. A white rose begins to bloom in her left palm. When the rose is fully formed, Diana gives it to Mercury, who handles it delicately.

"Mother Guardian," Mercury says, addressing Havah, "I need your blessing."

"Of course, Mercury," Havah says, "of course."

Mercury holds out his hand and Havah puts her hand in his. Mercury gently lays the white rose on top of the ashes.

"Nothing is ever truly lost," Havah and Mercury say in unison, "let great beauty rise from ashes."

Chapter 6:

Shake it Out

The ashes dance and twirl; an ascending spiral of grey, black and white. Slowly, the specks of ash light up. Tiny flames emerge like wood burning on a funeral pyre. A shrill sound reverberates through the Cosmic Womb. The flames grow larger and larger till a firebird takes shape. A breath-taking phoenix rises from the ashes, its light is bright and hot, rivalling that of the Sun.

"With death, there is always rebirth," Mercury and Havah say together.

The phoenix continues growing and growing till it engulfs the entire room, purifying and cleansing the Cosmic Womb in which it has been resurrected. All present fall to their knees in awe of the firebird that has the power to continuously renew itself. The phoenix flaps its wings, its fiery feathers a spectacular display of red, orange, and yellow.

The Sun raises his head and looks at the phoenix with reverence.

"Beloved cousin," the Sun says. "We were born of the same fire. I give life to all Little Lights, whilst you bring them back from the abyss. Grant this Little Light the gift of life again."

The firebird rises and rises, its form shifting and swaying. The orange-yellow-red hues morph into a deep dark red. A winged, horned, four-legged dragon appears where the phoenix once was.

"Greetings," a proud voice says.

Mercury and Havah let go of each other's hands. They stare at the marvelous creature in front of them. There is something captivating, alluring and decadent about him; the rebel of the cosmos.

"Hello, Rahu," Dag says, with a grin. "Pleasure to have you back."

"The pleasure is all mine," Rahu says.

"The pleasures of all creation have always been yours," Diana says with a poorly veiled hint of irritation.

"Now, now, Diana," Rahu says. "After all this time, don't tell me you're still jealous."

"I can't possibly be jealous of you and your demon sister," Diana says.

"I suppose by now it is futile to tell you that we are not demons. After all these cycles, you still resist my very existence, even though you know full well that without me, humanity will never evolve or reach its true potential. Besides… if you and the Sun never had your secret forbidden tryst, Ketu and I would not be here."

"You…," the Sun says. "How dare you speak to Diana in that way!"

"Now, now, Surya," Rahu mocks. "Must the truth offend you so?"

"It is because of you that Little Lights suffer," Diana barks.

Rahu laughs sarcastically. After all this time, the enmity between them remains. Everything in creation has its cost.

"The Moon is the earth's very own Mother," Rahu says sardonically, "watching over mankind and protecting it from fulfilling its own destiny. But humanity deserves better. No soul ever grows into its full majesty if it is pampered from the very hardships it needs to grow. No child, no matter how loved, can remain in its mother's arms forever. I expected more from you, Diana, beloved Moon in Aries. To think those on earth revere you as the Warrior Goddess. It will be better for the both of us if you assist me in my mission instead of thwarting my path."

"He is right," Havah says, looking at Diana.

"But…," Diana says.

"I request you to do as he asks," Havah cuts her off in a quietly authoritative voice.

Dag smiles to himself. That was no request, but an order. For no planet or luminary can ever refuse the Mother Guardian of the Lore. Not even Dag himself can say no to one of Havah's 'requests'.

"Do I have your allegiance?" Rahu asks, giving Diana a haughty secret smile.

Diana looks at the Sun. How can the two great luminaries of the solar system feel so powerless in front of some illusion that takes the shape of a dragon?

"We must do what is right for Liora," the Sun says, accepting the hard truth.

Diana nods. Even a warrior goddess must accept that there are battles that can't be won.

"You have my allegiance," Diana says.

"Very well, then," Rahu says with a victorious smile.

Ω

"Who are you?" the Little Light asks. "The others I recognized, but you... you seem... foreign."

Rahu turns around to take a good look at the Little Light. Although the Little Light does not know him, he knows her well. He knows her desires and destiny like they are his very own. After all, when humanity ascends, so does Rahu. Each soul that fulfils its life task makes Rahu stronger.

"There is something of Ketu somewhere in you," the Little Light says, "and yet, you seem… nothing like her."

"Yes, Little Light," Rahu says, "if Ketu is karma, then I am dharma."

"Dharma?"

"Ketu and I were once one. We were split in half so that humanity could exist and ascend. I am the light. And Ketu is my shadow. I cannot exist without her, nor she without me. She forces mankind to experience great dissatisfaction so that they will eventually turn to me – and take the path that will bring them true bliss.

"Growing up is never easy. It is always painful, scary, full of hard choices, and fraught with difficulties – but at the end of it you realize that those experiences made you wiser, and brought you closer to your truth."

The Little Light looks at Rahu and smiles.

"Perhaps you are right, Great Dragon," the Little Light says. "But tell me, why do the others dislike you so?"

"Because I am different. I am no great luminary. I am not a planet. As far as they are concerned, my sister and I should not exist. We are the outcasts of the cosmos. In your own life, you will learn that it is not easy being different, that it's not easy to walk a lonely path. But through that journey you will learn that humanity evolves because of those who are unafraid to chart their own course."

"You are as magnificent as you are wise, Great Dragon."

Rahu grins, pleased with himself. He has ushered many Little Lights through the Cosmic Womb. It is his duty to push souls into living out their highest potential on earth.

Unfortunately, many souls do not step up to their soul task. After all, once the soul inhabits a human body it grows fearful of the unknown. Instead of embracing its true purpose, the soul runs from its own destiny, thinking that if it avoids it long enough those longings, those yearnings will just disappear. Some souls take lifetimes to achieve their soul task. Other souls slip further and further into the abyss until they have nowhere left to go.

"So what is my destiny?" the Little Light asks.

"It is not every day I meet a Little Light that is so wise. I see it... Your soul is old, tired, and weary. But still, your light shines with an incredible depth and warmth. You know how humanity suffers, yet you know this suffering is necessary. You understand how humanity will never change unless it experiences great darkness. You know full well how hard it is for light to fight the shadows, for one cannot exist without the other."

"Is my soul up to this task?" the Little Light asks.

"You chose this life task. The other Celestial Beings and I can only bestow gifts and gently guide you towards the realization of your destiny. We do not have the power to choose life tasks. That decision has always belonged to the Great Light and the Little Lights."

The Little Light ponders Rahu's words. For some reason, she trusts Rahu. She trusts that he is the key to some unknown door that will lead to the fulfilment of the desire that brought her to the Cosmic Womb.

"I accept your guidance," the Little Light says.

"You cannot accept me without accepting my sister," Rahu says. "Do you understand?"

"I do."

"Very well."

Rahu takes a deep breath. As the heat rises through him, his being fills with desire born of the Great Light. When he can take no more, he gently exhales; the flames emanating from him engulf the whole Cosmic Womb in premonitions of what might one day be.

Ω

Maya, a voice whispers. Maya. It's time. Time for you to emerge from the womb.

It's approximately midday. The Sun is at the highest point in the sky. The rest of the planets watch silently, as the Little Light manifests itself into the physical world of matter.

"It's a girl," the doctor says.

Not that he had to. The gender of the baby was known well before it was born. After the nurses cut the umbilical cord, they hand the baby to the mother who feeds her for the very first time. Despite the pain of the labor, the Mother feels a deep love growing inside her for the baby that she brought into this world. It is like I loved you well before you were born, she thinks. Perhaps we were tied together in a previous life.

A black owl with turquoise eyes silently sweeps into the room. Only the baby can see it.

"I am Pirouzeh," the Owl says. "The spirit guide of your paternal ancestors. I am here to guide you in this world so that you may fulfil your destiny. It is not a path that has been laid out for you, but one that you will have to create on your own."

The baby looks at the owl and blinks. The journey from the Cosmic Womb to the physical world is a painful one for the Mother and for the Little Light itself.

"You have inherited a great legacy," Pirouzeh says, "but by the time you are old enough to inherit it, the old ways will have turned to dust.

"Know that you have been born into this world so that you can bring forth a new legacy – one that will survive for generations to

come. To help you in this task, you will meet your twin when the time is right. You may not recognize him, but he will recognize you. Together, you will bring forth a new age for all mankind.

"But for now, sleep, little one."

The baby closes its eyes and falls asleep.

Maya, a voice whispers. Maya.

Your time has come.

Ω

Rahu puts out the flame. The Little Light scratches her eyes and shakes her head.

"What was that?" the Little Light asks.

"A prophecy," Rahu says. "A glimpse into the future."

"What's a prophecy?"

"It is a prediction of what the future may bring. However, it is not what might come to pass."

Rahu breathes fire again, his physical form morphing from a dragon to a man. Like Ketu, he is an illusion without a physical body. Rahu wears a long red robe emblazoned with two circling black dragons. A gold belt is wrapped around his waist. His long straight hair hangs loosely around his shoulders. His eyes are dark and piercing, the shadows of his eyes painted red. He holds a long gold wand in his right hand.

"For all this talk of destiny and desire," Ketu says, "it is ultimately free will that decides the fate of man. The choices may be predetermined, but the choice is not."

"Hello to you too, sister," Rahu says with a naughty gleam in his eye.

"What legacy am I to build?" the Little Light asks.

"We will have to wait till the others get here before we can answer that question," Ketu says. "But before that happens, you will need to accept your karma and all that it holds."

The Little Light looks over at Dag.

"Do you promise to watch over me?" the Little Light asks.

"Always," Dag says. "Fear not, Little Light. You are never alone. We will forever be your celestial companions. But you will meet Little Lights like you who will also lend a hand and assist you should you ever need it. You have it in you to bear your pain so that you may live again."

The Little Light looks around the Cosmic Womb. She hesitates, but a force greater than herself urges her on. "I accept my destiny," she says, resolute.

"Take my hand," Ketu says.

The Little Light willingly puts her hand in Ketu's.

"Before you can forget, you must remember," Ketu says. "And before you can ascend, you must descend."

Ketu morphs into a slender silver serpent and enters the Little Light's body at the base of her spine. The Little Light shrieks and yells out in agony – so many memories, so many incarnations, so much pain, so much joy, so much happiness, so much loss, so much… The million shades of life's countless past experiences take hold of Little Light. Flashbacks, feelings, memories of other Little Lights with unfinished business. Debts paid. Debts yet to be repaid. The silver serpent coils from the base of the spine and descends into the ground.

The Little Light cries out in unbearable desperation. The luminaries have seen this scene countless times, but still they avert their eyes. The Mother and Father Guardian watch, for they are required to witness this moment.

It is the Lore. No Little Light must ever be alone in this terrible moment of despair.

The Little Light's astral body turns grey as it revisits the past. Screams – the unabashed sound of pure anguish and heartache – echo through the Cosmic Womb. Havah sheds a tear, for she knows all too well how attachments from past lives can linger; how souls can hold onto each other and refuse to let go; how souls can attach themselves and leave tiny pieces of their own light in other Little Lights.

The Little Light cries out – for all that has been lost in previous incarnations, and for all that will be lost in the next. Ketu forces Little Light to experience the Dark Night of the Soul so that it can finally detach itself from it. The Little Light wails and weeps uncontrollably.

"That's enough," Rahu says finally, wiping the tears in his eyes. "I can't take anymore."

Beneath the Little Light's feet there is a black hole that threatens to suck her in. The fiery temperament of the Little Light is gone; all that's left is a hollow shell of despair.

"I am all alone in the world," the Little Light says. "All alone. In a cold, dark world where no one cares. Where there is no love, no light, no meaning. Where everything we cherish and love, we will one day lose."

Havah swallows hard and clenches her fist. She feels the Little Light's feelings as though they were her own. Havah tries hard to stop herself from sobbing openly.

Dag places a hand on her shoulder. His feelings are not too far from hers, but he contains himself. All good mothers hurt when they watch their children suffer.

Even Diana, the Warrior Goddess, struggles to maintain composure.

Rahu changes his form into the Red Dragon once more. He enters the Little Light at the base of her spine as Ketu did. A red fire ignites, warming Little Light's now grey body. Rahu slowly coils, ascending upwards, vertebrae by vertebrae. The Little Light stops crying out. Her pain morphs into quiet determination as her body emits flashes of red. She trembles with fear. So much greatness, so much power, so many unrealized accomplishments – all latent in one body till the moment it will be fully realized. Rahu keeps ascending, coiling slowly till it reaches the top of Little Light's crown.

The Little Light's eyes flicker open, determined and proud. For what is done cannot be undone, but its energy can be transformed into something new. The phoenix re-emerges above the Cosmic Womb, its colossal form engulfing and purifying all that has been.

"With death, there is always rebirth," the phoenix says before vanishing once more.

The descending Ketu ascends from the black hole and steadily wraps itself around Rahu. Together, they are stronger than they were alone. Together, they merge the past and future into the present moment.

The Little Light stretches out her arms in victory. The hidden latent energy of Rahu and Ketu reverberating through her astral body. The silver and red helix inextricably entwined; karma and dharma, light and shadow.

Rahu and Ketu depart from Little Light's body. They have left a piece of their collective essences inside her. Their work is now complete.

"It is as it was written," Dag whispers. "It is as it was written. It is futile to resist."

Chapter 7:

Have a Little Faith in Me

"What did I miss?" a chirpy, enduringly up-beat and slightly annoying voice says.

"If it isn't the eternal optimist." Mercury grins, relieved that she's here to lighten the atmosphere. "Welcome back, Jupiter."

"Good to be back and see the extended family!" Jupiter says. "I'm always happy to see you lot. Mercury, looking dashing as always! You've grown into a fine young man."

"Thank you," Mercury says, "for seeing what my father never does."

"There, there, Mercury," Jupiter says. "You know Papa always has your best interests at heart. But I suppose it's wise I don't interfere in your domestic matters too much. I'll just subtly change the topic, if you don't mind..."

Jupiter leans in to give Mercury a quick peck on the cheek. Mercury smiles broadly, flashing his perfect teeth.

"I see my own father Saturn is not here yet," Jupiter says. "How delightful! He has a way of making things heavy and somber. Don't tell him I said that — although I have a sneaking suspicion he knows how I feel. Not that he cares. As if parents ever listen to their children."

Everyone laughs. Jupiter has always had a way of infusing optimism into the direst of circumstances. Little Lights blessed by Jupiter have the ability to see the silver lining in the greyest of clouds.

"The Great Guru," Diana says as she reaches forward to embrace Jupiter. "The Cosmic Teacher of Light."

"Looking beautiful as always, Diana," Jupiter says, giving her a kiss on the cheek. "Moon in Aries, I see. A resilient mind for a special Little Light. I approve.

"And you're as eternally ravishing as I remember, Havah."

"Flatterer," Havah says, smiling in spite of herself.

"And Dag," Jupiter says, "looking mighty fine for a man your age. I'd hope for your good genes, if I even had genes!"

"Thank you always for your kind words," Dag says smiling.

"And they say I'm the one with the quicksilver tongue," Mercury scoffs. "Can I get another peck on the cheek?"

Jupiter leans forward and kisses Mercury again. Mercury looks mighty pleased with himself.

"And if it isn't Ketu herself," Jupiter says, "I can't hug you, as you're a shadow, but it's nice to see you all the same. Where is your other half? Oh, there you are Rahu. I much prefer you when you're a dragon. You make a pretty cool dragon, if I may say so myself. And if you don't mind, I'd love to see you morph into a dragon. Oh, pretty please."

"Jupiter," Rahu sighs, exasperated, "I don't know what's worse; your self-righteous way of being a know-it-all, or your eternal optimism that spreads like an infection to those of us who'd much prefer being cynics."

"Oh, Rahu," Jupiter says, "you know you love me."

"I really don't..."

"Has anyone ever told you that you have the loveliest hair? If you don't mind, I'd just like to run my fingers through it..."

"Don't you dare!"

Rahu flicks Jupiter off as she leans in to touch him, but she persists.

"Oh, just a teeny touch..." Jupiter says.

"Get away from me!" Rahu slaps her hand away.

"But we're family!"

Rahu shakes his head and places his hand on his forehead.

"Whenever I see you," Rahu says, "I remember why humans on earth hate family gatherings."

"Ok, forget the hair. How about I pinch your cheeks instead? Ok well, maybe you're past the age for that. A hug? What do you think? Yes, a hug will work quite nicely."

Jupiter inches closer to Rahu, who quickly transforms to his dragon form before she has the chance to touch him.

"Of all the Celestial Beings," Rahu says, "you have got to be the most annoying."

"Oh, thank you so much for morphing into a dragon just for me! You're the best, Rahu, simply the best. In fact, of everyone, I think I might just love you the most. And don't worry about jealousy, I have a feeling the rest of them don't mind. I've always wanted my own baby dragon."

Rahu takes a deep breath in. He is unnerved by Jupiter's tenderness. Affection is not an emotion that he's used to receiving.

"Every time you're near me," Rahu says. "I wish I were deaf."

"Oh, Rahu, you need not run from your feelings for me. I know you love me as much as I love you!"

"It's like you don't hear a word I say."

Jupiter walks towards Rahu and holds his face in her hands.

"You're the best, most beautiful, most magnificent Red Dragon in the world," Jupiter says. "Your presence in the world makes it a better place. Some of the others may not like you, but I want you to know I have deep stores of affection for you."

Rahu shakes his head and sits down; silent, fed up, and frustrated. If there's one Celestial Being that can tame the fire in Rahu's heart, it's Jupiter.

Everyone present laughs. They are glad to see Jupiter. They needed her cheerful presence after everything they'd just witnessed.

"You are the Great Guru," the Little Light says. "We have met before, but you were different, then. If my memories serve me right, you were a man!"

Jupiter laughs. Like Mercury, Jupiter can take on two physical forms – one masculine, one feminine. Her masculine side rules over the constellation of Sagittarius, and her feminine side rules over the constellation of Pisces.

"Yes, Little Light," Jupiter says. "I can be a man, too. But for now, I am a lady."

"The High Priestess herself," Mercury says, smiling.

Whilst Mercury has never understood the deep waters of Pisces, he has always regarded Jupiter with a quiet respect. She is the big sister he never had and secretly looks up to. Jupiter has forever brought a certain happiness and light to these planet parties. Without her, the universe would be a cold and harsh place.

Jupiter wears a long, ocean blue dress embroidered with two fishes swimming in opposite directions. On her forehead rests a headpiece made of cream-colored pearls. She is wrapped in a cloak of owl feathers; a gift from her father Saturn, to honor her deep wisdom.

"You are deeply blessed, Little Light," Mercury says.

"Why?" the Little Light asks.

"You are born with a Jupiter in Pisces."

"Ahem... Ahem...," the Sun says, interrupting.

"What is it, dad?" Mercury looks back at him, irritated.

"Just earlier you said you hated being in Pisces, and how it makes you feel like an emotional basket case and now you—"

Mercury grins and pretends to listen. He deeply enjoys annoying his father. When he was younger, he used to talk back, fight back a little more. But these days, he lets his father go on and on. He nods in agreement while secretly daydreaming of other, more important matters.

"Are you listening to me?" the Sun asks.

"No," Mercury replies with a secret smile. "But that never stops you from lecturing me anyway."

"This boy, I tell you," the Sun says, angrily. "He never shows me any respect."

"Will you two stop bickering?" the Little Light says.

Dag suddenly erupts in laughter, smacking his knee.

"The Little Light is already tired of your arguments," Dag says, slightly tearing up from the laughter. "Imagine Havah and I having to put up with this ridiculous nonsense each time we usher a soul into the world."

"I enjoy their arguments," Rahu says slyly. "What's life without a little conflict?"

"Oh, my little baby dragon Rahu," Jupiter says. "How I love the sound of your bellowing voice."

"How dare you call me a baby dragon!"

"You're all warm and cuddly," Jupiter says.

"I am hot and fiery, you annoying optimist with rose-tinted glasses! Don't you ever get sick of smothering me with your unwanted affection?"

"Oh, c'mon, baby Rahu. Deep down you know you want nothing more than to be loved."

"STOP CALLING ME BABY RAHU!"

Everyone present in the Cosmic Womb laughs. They cry tears of joy at the sheer ridiculousness of the moment. Jupiter has always had a way of taming the wildest of hearts with her tenderness.

"Baby Rahu," Ketu says. "It has a nice ring to it."

"You're one of them!" Rahu says.

Rahu breathes fire across the room, startling everyone into silence.

"This is one dysfunctional cosmic family," the Little Light says.

"As above, so below, Little Light," Mercury says. "As above, so below."

"Wise words, Mercury," Havah says. "Wise words."

"I have my moments." Mercury smiles, mighty pleased with himself.

"Jupiter in Pisces," the Little Light says. "What does it mean to be born with a Jupiter in Pisces?"

"You are born with lady luck on your side," Rahu says grudgingly.

Jupiter smiles and taps Rahu on the head. Rahu responds with a slight growl, much to Jupiter's glee. Jupiter turns her gaze to the Little Light.

"There's someone very special I'd like you to meet, Little Light," Jupiter says. "Havah, you know what you need to do."

Havah nods. She takes a deep breath. The pupils of her eyeballs turn white. She enters the invisible realm that interacts with mankind's physical reality. There are very few humans who can see this invisible realm in their waking hours. Perhaps that is for the best – if they could, they'd go mad.

"I summon Pirouzeh," Havah says. "The Spirit Animal of the Owl Clan."

A few moments pass. A black bird sweeps into the Cosmic Womb. Its feathers make no noise. Its presence makes no grand entrance. The proud and independent owl slowly opens its eyelids, revealing intense turquoise eyes that see everything, know everything.

"Greetings, Havah." Pirouzeh speaks with a deliberate cadence. "And my deepest regards to the fellow Celestial Beings as well. Why have you summoned me? I am not usually privy to these planet parties – not that I mind being here. The Cosmic Womb is such a terribly beautiful place, especially when compared to life on earth."

"It is I who asked Havah," Jupiter says. "Greetings, Pirouzeh."

"Well, well…" Pirouzeh says, "if it isn't the great gas planet. The one that nearly became a star herself and… failed. Who would have thought that the largest planet of the Celestial Beings is actually … a failed star?"

"There can only be one star," the Sun says proudly. The Sun has never been as fond of Jupiter as the others, but he can't say he particularly dislikes her either. Nevertheless, the Sun has always believed that she should know her place… as number two.

"Big deal," Pirouzeh says, unimpressed. "A medium-sized star in one of the universe's many galaxies. I take it you're still giving the same sermons you used to, even though you're fully aware that no one listens and quite frankly, no one gives a damn."

Mercury raises his eyebrows. He has never seen anyone speak to the Sun in that way. Although he knows Pirouzeh is right, a part of him feels irritated that someone would speak so casually to his father.

"I thought you said that Jupiter in Pisces signified good luck," the Little Light says. "This doesn't seem lucky at all."

"Maya," Pirouzeh says, her voice softening. "Is it really you?"

"Why do you call me that?" the Little Light asks. "Why did you call me that in the prophecy I saw earlier?"

"That will be your name in your next incarnation. I have foreseen it. I hope you were not offended by my sharp tongue. I am a solitary bird that hunts alone. As beautiful as the Cosmic Womb is, I can't say I'm particularly thrilled to be at this party, even if it is one hosted by the Nine Great Celestial Beings."

"Who are you? Do I know you? Unlike the others, I feel that we have never met."

"I am your spirit animal. I once lived in the physical world, but I have since passed on. Unlike the Celestial Beings, I can move between the worlds of men and spirit at will. I will be your guide once you are born. I promise to guide you, just as I once guided your ancestors."

"My ancestors?"

"Yes…your genetic lineage, past and present. It is a powerful family, but not an easy one to be born into. The Owl Clan's dictum is *takya, takha* – throne or coffin. Win, no matter what the cost.

"Your ancestors were ruthless warriors – some might even say that they were the greatest warriors the world has ever seen. They were fearless, courageous, and bold. They ventured out into the world and were never afraid to claim what they thought was rightfully theirs."

The Little Light observes Pirouzeh quizzically. It is hard for The Little Light to fully comprehend what her spirit animal is telling her. The world of men feels far away from the bliss she felt when she emerged from the Great Light and made her journey into the Cosmic Womb.

"I am not destined to be a warrior," the Little Light says.

"I am aware." Pirouzeh nods. "But you will have to learn to fight and fend for yourself till your first Saturn Return. I will guide you till then."

"My first Saturn Return?"

"I will be your spirit animal till you turn 31 in human years. Upon the completion of your Saturn Return, you will receive a new spirit animal to guide you. It is not an easy life your soul has chosen to be born into, but it will all make sense when you finally see the light at the end of the tunnel."

Jupiter and Havah exchange a quick glance. They both know that not all souls survive infancy, let alone make it through their Saturn Return unscathed. There is a lot that can go wrong. If the Little Light forsakes its true soul mission, then it will be sometime before it gets back on track. That is a risk Jupiter cannot afford to take.

"Rahu," Jupiter says, her usual cheerful optimism gone, "I need you."

"Glad to be of service, my lady," Rahu says.

"I'm sorry I teased you earlier," Jupiter says, suddenly serious.

"No apology necessary. You are the big sister I never had."

"Promise me you will make sure that Little Light sees the light at the end of the tunnel. I fear it might all be too much for her to bear and she might get lost along the way."

"I promise."

"Thank you."

The truth is, Rahu had no choice but to promise. Jupiter was selected by the Great Light itself to pass down its teachings. To deny what Jupiter asks would be to deny the Great Light.

"Dag and Havah," Jupiter says, "promise me that you will go down to earth and intervene in the event of irreversible misfortune. I know that hardships cannot be entirely avoided, but promise me that Little Light will never lose her faith in the Great Light or in humanity's larger purpose."

"We promise," Havah and Dag say.

"Mercury," Jupiter says, "promise me that you will teach her all the business and political acumen necessary to survive. But under no circumstances are you allowed to let her believe that her true calling lies in the business world."

"I promise," Mercury says in a rare display of maturity.

"Diana," Jupiter says, "promise me that you will allow her mind to unleash its wrath when it comes to defeating her enemies. Show her that it is not wrong to vanquish those who try to harm her."

"I promise," Diana says.

"And Ketu," Jupiter says, "promise me that other Little Lights she has assisted in previous lifetimes will come to help her now."

"I promise."

Jupiter sighs. The Celestial Beings may all have agreed to help, but she needs someone down on the ground. It is easy for Little Lights to forget the promises made in the Cosmic Womb once they are born. After all, this place is a vortex before time. The physical world has its own set of laws that are entirely different to life in the Cosmos, even though the two are inextricably interconnected.

"And Pirouzeh," Jupiter says finally, "promise me that she will come to no great harm by her kin."

"Jupiter…," Pirouzeh says. "You ask too much. Throne or coffin. It is their way."

"Promise me," Jupiter barks. "You know as well as I do that that was not a request!"

"How dare you speak to me in that way!"

"I am the High Priestess, I rule over the bridge between the spiritual and material worlds, it would not be wise to disobey me."

"It is not in my nature to take orders. I am an owl. In my heart of hearts, I am a solitary creature. I belong to no one."

Jupiter stares into Pirouzeh's eyes, her cheerful disposition gone, "You will do as I ask."

"I refuse," Pirouzeh says firmly.

"You cannot refuse me!" Jupiter yells.

All the Celestial Beings take a step back. Mercury taps his foot lightly. Pirouzeh remains steadfast. Her eyes show no sign of fear.

"Free will," Pirouzeh says unflustered. "It is embedded into the design of this universe. I do not have to do as you ask."

"You have spent too much time in the world of men and you have forgotten your true purpose, you insolent creature!"

"Do not take that tone with me. The Celestial Beings may not deny you, but I can. It is the Lore."

Jupiter glares at Pirouzeh with deep-seated spite. Despite Jupiter's ordinarily cheerful disposition, the Celestial Beings know that she is not a woman to be trifled with. But owls are solitary creatures, they spend so much time alone that they sometimes forget how to interact with beings more powerful than themselves. They forget that they are a part of the world and it is a part of them.

Jupiter removes a pearl from her headpiece and flings it at Pirouzeh. Diana's jaw widens in horror. The pearl lands on Pirouzeh's forehead, marking it. The black bird shrieks and squeals, its feathers fluttering uncontrollably.

"I bestow you, Pirouzeh," Jupiter says, "with the gift of compassion. With the same compassion that created the human experience. I temper your unparalleled intelligence with the ability to feel the emotions of others as if they were your own. With time, you will grow to love this Little Light. Her suffering will be your suffering. Her pain will be your pain. Her joys will be your joys. Her happiness will be your happiness. I gift you, Pirouzeh. I gift you."

Pirouzeh grows silent. Her eyes remain shut. Moments pass. Havah inquisitively looks at the bird with furrowed brows.

"Pirouzeh," Havah says. "Are you still with us? We need you, wise one. We cannot do this without you."

Pirouzeh unwillingly opens her all-seeing eyes. Her head gently turns, her deep penetrating eyes intensely observe each Celestial Being. She flies around the Cosmic Womb before settling on the Little Light's shoulder.

"Forgive me, Great Guru," Pirouzeh says, "I have not forgotten the Great Light, nor the compassion that created me. I have spent too much time in the world of men; a world that has evolved materially and devolved spiritually, a world of unspeakable horrors."

Pirouzeh closes her eyes and hangs her head down.

"I have seen too much," Pirouzeh says with heaviness in her voice. "I am weary and tired."

Pirouzeh's turquoise eyes turn grey.

"I wish to weep," Pirouzeh says. "There have been many times over the course of the Owl Clan's history where I have wished to weep. But we spirit animals may not weep. It is the Lore."

The Little Light reaches forward to stroke Pirouzeh but then instinctively stops herself.

"I appreciate the gesture, Little Light," Pirouzeh says, as her eyes change back to turquoise. "You have no idea how long I have awaited your arrival. Being in your presence is a great honor."

"Pirouzeh," Jupiter says with guilt in her voice. "You have held it all inside all these years. I did not know…"

"Please," Pirouzeh says. "Spare me the sympathy. I cannot bear it."

Jupiter reaches forward to stroke Pirouzeh in an attempt to comfort her.

"I do not wish to be touched," Pirouzeh says.

Jupiter nods her head and retreats.

"Maya," Pirouzeh says. "I promise to watch over you, always. No great harm will come to you of your kin."

"Thank you, Pirouzeh," the Little Light says. "Thank you."

"Pirouzeh…," Jupiter says with deep remorse in her voice. "You should not have disobeyed me. I did not want to do that…"

"It is not in an owl's nature to obey," Pirouzeh says. "I exercised my free will. And I willingly paid the price. I received a 'gift' from the High Priestess that will alter the course of the vengeful Owl Clan forever. You honor me, Great Guru. You honor me. After all, it is not just Maya I watch over, but all those of her lineage – past, present and future."

"I see," Jupiter says. "You are indeed as wise as they say. I unwittingly gave you what you wanted. The Owl Clan was once destined to be the wisest clan that ever walked the earth. What happened?"

"Too much bloodshed. It can turn the warmest of hearts cold and vengeful. Humans have grown greedy. Their unrestrained self-interest forces them to take more from Mother Earth than they need."

"Is it true?" Jupiter asks.

"It is true," Diana says with a sigh. "I have watched over the earth and pulled on its tides since the dawn of time. I'm afraid mankind can no longer be trusted to fulfil its destiny."

"What happened to humans? How did this happen?" Jupiter asks.

"Free will," Pirouzeh says. "And the enormous suffering that ensued from it."

"Is humanity's suffering really that great?" Jupiter asks.

"It is unbearable to watch them," Diana says. "To watch over them. They ache, but they do not know what they ache for. They cry, but they do not know what is causing the pain. They pray to the Creator, not knowing the Creator lives inside them. They have forgotten, Jupiter. They have forgotten."

"Will I forget this incredible place?" the Little Light asks as she strokes Pirouzeh behind the head.

Owls ordinarily do not like to be stroked, but Pirouzeh allows herself to be touched. Despite their independent nature, owls are deeply devoted to those who've earned their affection.

"Never, Little Light," Jupiter says. "I, the High Priestess of the Celestial Beings, grant you the teachings of the Great Light. You will be born with great intuition and the rare ability to see into the hearts of all men. You will be a channel for the creative force that created this universe and pervades all things.

"I cannot change the ways of mankind. But I can provide you with safe passage to survive life's darkest days and emerge untouched, unscarred, and untarnished.

"Of this, you have my promise."

"It is as it was written," Dag says. "No matter what happens, it always is as it was written. Mankind always finds its Soul Star again."

Chapter 8:

Kiss from a Rose

"**F**ellow Celestial Beings," a sensual and melodious voice whispers. "How lovely to see you all gathered here."

The sweet subtle scent of freshly-cut roses meanders through the Cosmic Womb. The Celestial Beings get a whiff and are momentarily disarmed. Even those who are ordinarily steadfast can't contain themselves. They are all briefly under her spell... till they regain their senses. She is incredibly beautiful in a way that only a woman can be.

"The morning and evening star herself," Mercury says tenderly, still enamored.

"She is hardly a star," Pirouzeh says with unrepressed boredom. "But a rocky planet, like the earth, Mars, and Mercury. Poets may romanticize her, but there is no reason why the rest of us should."

"You're absolutely right, Pirouzeh," the Sun says, smiling.

"Don't be so proud of yourself," Pirouzeh retorts harshly. "You medium-sized, middle-aged, pompous luminary."

"Show me some respect, you disrespectful owl."

"I will the day you show some humility, you self-centered egomaniac. I'm so glad I rarely attend these planet parties. I don't know how the others can stand you. You really are a royal pain in the—"

"Pirouzeh," Diana says sternly. "Let it go. Please."

The owl blinks her eyes three times and then turns her head 270 degrees.

"You're lucky my kind revere you, Diana," Pirouzeh says. "It is your mysterious ways that make you so magnificent."

Diana smiles. Mothers are rarely appreciated in this way. Once a woman becomes a mother, she ceases to be the maiden she once was. The little girl must die so that the grown woman may be live. It is the Lore.

"If I am the earth's mother," Diana says, "then you are its sister. Perhaps even its twin. Greetings, Venus."

"Greetings, Diana," Venus says. "Like you, I appear to wax and wane to earth dwellers. I am your sister as much as I am the earth's."

"The world reveres your great beauty as it does no other. You have, and will always be, the Queen of the Sky."

"Thank you for your kind words, Diana."

Venus wears a long, gold lace evening gown. Her physical form demands the uninterrupted attention of everyone in the room. She is stunning and incredibly pleasing to the eye. Men are spellbound in her presence, whilst women can't help but feel an unmistakable stab of jealousy. Venus' long, dark, luscious hair hangs loosely around her waist. Her green eyes flutter lightly. Her movements are soft and graceful. She is the lady of the heavens, marking the dusk and dawn with her presence.

"The eternal maiden of the cosmos," Mercury says.

"Hardly," Jupiter says, rolling her eyes. "She is my mother."

Venus throws her head back and laughs. Unlike the Moon, she remains unmarked by motherhood. She is the only Celestial Being who looks as beautiful as she did many cycles ago. There are many that say she only gets more beautiful with the passing of time.

"Hello, my daughter," Venus says embracing Jupiter. "Where's papa?"

"You know how he is," Jupiter says, "slow, steady, and always the last to arrive. He is not known for his punctuality."

Everyone present laughs.

"Indeed," Dag says. "Saturn, the Lord of Time, is forever late."

"And yet," Havah says, "he never ceases to show up at exactly the right moment."

"Enough about Saturn," the Sun says with jealousy in his tone.

Dag raises an eyebrow. The rivalry between the two great fathers of the cosmos is well-known. But then again, Saturn is the only one who can stand up to the Sun as its equal.

"Anyways," Mercury says, changing the topic. "We're all dying to know. Is Little Light blessed by you?"

"In a sense," Venus says smiling secretly.

Venus is the 'woman' in every woman. She represents the part of the woman that shines... or diminishes... when she is in love. Women blessed by Venus have that little something that commands attention by virtue of its aesthetic beauty.

"Venus," Diana says, "in which constellation are you?"

"Capricorn."

The constellation of Capricorn is ruled by Saturn, Venus' husband.

"The woman who gets better with time," Havah says. "Marries late and is steadfast and stable in love."

"If and when she falls in love," Rahu says, smiling. "Venus in Capricorn... A cold and somewhat cruel lover that never surrenders its heart till its affection is earned. I approve..."

"But that's not the whole story," Venus says. "I was given this whilst I journeyed here."

In Venus' hand is a flaming red feather from the phoenix.

"A gift from the phoenix!" Jupiter says. "How lovely! May I touch it?"

"You most certainly may not," Venus retorts.

Jupiter pouts, smiling cheekily. She extends a hand in an attempt to touch the feather but Venus smacks her hand away.

"Don't make me scold you," Venus says. "Nagging makes me feel rather unattractive."

"And no one could possibly be more attractive than you," the Sun mocks.

"All children love to be scolded by their parents," Mercury says. "It is one of the joys of being a child – to be naughty, and get scolded for it."

"You kids really should start acting like grownups," the Sun says. "You're not children anymore."

"Well...," Mercury says cheekily, "what's the point of acting like a grownup if we will always be children in our parents' eyes?"

"Well-played, Mercury," Dag says. "He has a point."

"How dare you talk back again?" the Sun says. "Don't you know that—"

"Yes, we all know," Pirouzeh says with contempt. "I am the superstar of the cosmos. The breadwinner. The father, the one that shines all day and gives humans skin cancer. There can be too much of a good thing, great Sun."

"You disrespectful owl!" the Sun says.

Pirouzeh smirks. "I'm curious to hear how many times you can say the word 'disrespectful' in the course of one planet party..."

"You dis..err...erm... you... disgraceful owl!"

Pirouzeh laughs, her hoots echoing through the Cosmic Womb. Mercury purses his lips to stop himself from laughing.

"I know you," the Little Light says interrupting, glaring at Venus. "I saw you. Earlier. When Ketu took me into the abyss."

Venus turns to look at the Little Light. *Yes, I remember this Little Light. I blessed her in her last incarnation and in many incarnations before that.* Venus is taken aback by the Little Light's anger. Most of mankind venerate Venus and would do anything for her gifts.

"Why do you look at me with such animosity?" Venus asks. "After all, I have given you everything."

"You…," the Little Light says with anger. "You gave me everything except my self-respect and independence."

Dag frowns. He knows what the Little Light is referring to. There are very few who can see past Venus' charms; who can see the ugliness beneath the glamour; the hollow emptiness behind the beautiful façade; who can see the dirty games Venus is willing to play to get what she wants.

"Venus," Ketu interrupts. "How good to see you!"

"Old friend." Venus smiles. "Always a pleasure."

"You two are not friends," the Little Light says in disgust, "but allies."

"That's very perceptive of you," Dag says, impressed.

Not many Little Lights can see through Venus' alluring façade.

"Everything Venus ever gave me was empty," the Little Light says, as her usually upbeat voice betrays an unbecoming bitterness. "A picture-perfect life that was broken underneath…"

"C'mon," Ketu says. "It wasn't all bad. You enjoyed riches that you didn't have to earn. You had the admiration of men and the jealousy of women. Most women would do anything to have that on the material plane."

"But it was all a lie," the Little Light says. "It was all an illusion."

A heavy silence hangs in the Cosmic Womb under the weight of what Little Light has said.

"You should be grateful for what I have given you," Venus says. "You had great relationships and created beautiful children."

"But I had to give up myself to create that life," the Little Light says. "At the end of the day, it was all a sham."

Dag sighs heavily. He knows that Venus' mesmerizing gifts always come at a price. All that shimmering stardust never lasts. It always leaves the recipient with a sense that something far more valuable was given up to receive it.

"What about the phoenix feather?" Mercury asks, hoping to change the topic.

Venus turns to acknowledge Mercury and grimaces. The Little Light has already been so greatly blessed by Jupiter. Any gift from Venus has always paled in comparison to the good luck, happiness, and joy that Jupiter can bestow. Deep down, Venus knows she can only ever give material pleasures, but not their true enjoyment.

"The Little Light will not find her twin till after her first Saturn Return," Venus says.

"My twin?" the Little Light asks.

"Yes. Your other half. The man whose destiny is inextricably entwined with yours. You are him and he is you."

"Why do I need a twin?"

Venus raises an eyebrow, surprised by the Little Light's remark. It is what everyone wishes for on some level – a person to share their life with, a significant other, a... partner. Someone to take away the hardships of life and make existence beautiful and comfortable.

"I see Diana has gifted you with her independence," Venus says. "She is the maiden that never marries. But that will not be your path. Everybody needs somebody, Little Light."

"I saw my past lives when I descended down Ketu's abyss. I don't want to come second anymore. I don't want to be number two. My partners have had all the limelight whilst I stood in the shadows. They loved me because of what I brought to *their* table. They did not love me for who I really was."

"What does it matter?" Venus asks.

"It matters to me. I do not want to be some pretty plaything on somebody's arm."

"Your heart will change after your first Saturn Return."

"I highly doubt it..." the Little Light says, resolute.

"Anyways," Mercury cuts in, "that still doesn't explain the feather."

"Little Light," Diana seconds to help Mercury. "When you have incarnated in human form, you will learn that there are many things in the world that feel like the real thing, but are merely fantasies. For instance, strong infatuations can feel like love, but they are merely passing reveries. Money can buy a house, but not a home. Knowledge can give great intelligence, but not wisdom. Marriage can bind two people together, but not their hearts.

"This phoenix feather has been gifted to you so that you may be reborn when the illusion you fall for comes crashing down."

"That's a great gift," the Little Light says.

"In a sense…" Venus gazes at the feather and then the Little Light. There's something she needs to say, but can't find the words. Ever since the dawn of time, she has only known and given beauty, luxury, opulence. Hard truths and life's challenges have never been her domain.

"Humans are fond of chasing illusions," Pirouzeh says. "They spend their whole lives building them up no matter how unhappy it makes them. You see, Little Light, Venus can give you all of life's pleasures, without the true bliss and satisfaction that comes with it. That's why the phoenix gifted you with this feather."

"Must you be so curt?" Venus asks, slightly hurt.

"We all know you're not one for reality checks," Pirouzeh says. "You spoilt, pampered Queen of the Skies."

"Pirouzeh," Jupiter says. "Please do not speak to my mother in that way."

Pirouzeh rolls her eyes, tired of all the nonsense that goes on at these planet parties. She wants to retreat into her nocturnal solitary life. Alas, the time is not yet.

"Do not chide Pirouzeh," Dag says, stepping in. "You know she speaks the truth, as she always has. Venus has always left Saturn to deal with the burdens and hardships of life. There is not much substance beneath that beauty. Still, we can't help but admire her, for Venus is truly irresistible."

"How kind of you to weigh in," Venus hisses. "I can always count on you to disguise a compliment as an insult."

"Unlike the others," Dag says, "I have never coveted your beauty, for I know the gifts you give fade. They do not have the ability to withstand the tests of time. Which is why the phoenix gave you the feather. You cannot be trusted to do anything right of your own accord!"

Havah puts a hand on Dag's shoulder. Venus has been the bane of his life since they met. Of all the Celestial Beings, she is the only one who can tempt men with illusions made of pure matter and set them down the wrong path.

"Little Light," Havah says. "Remember that true beauty lasts through the toughest of storms. There are many things in the world that are fleeting. You must learn to differentiate traps from opportunities. Your soul made a wise decision to choose Venus in Capricorn. You will not give your heart to any man who has not earned your love.

Perhaps that might delay finding your twin, but I believe it is for the best."

"You are all just jealous of my beauty," Venus says.

"Oh, what have we here?" Pirouzeh scoffs. "A rocky planet that thinks it's a star."

"Pirouzeh...," Jupiter says.

"Jupiter, has anyone ever told you that you're an insufferable mummy's girl?"

"I'm with you on that one," Rahu chimes in.

Pirouzeh meets Rahu's eyes. There is something similar about the two of them. They are both outcasts at this planet party, there for humanity's sake. The rest of the Celestial Beings are there on the Great Light's orders. Ketu, Rahu, Pirouzeh, and the Guardians of the Lore are the only ones who know first-hand how mankind suffers after it is torn away from the Great Light and given free will.

In Pirouzeh's company, Rahu realizes that he and his sister are not alone in the universe. That there are other renegades, just like him who know that the Lore must change, or it will die.

"My Baby Rahu," Jupiter says as she reaches forward to pat Rahu on the head.

Rahu breathes fire in her direction. "Do not patronize me, Jupiter. I know how the Little Light has suffered in silence through her previous incarnations. Most of you can't understand her yearnings and desires, but I can.

"In her next life, she will create a legacy that she can be proud of. Her majesty will no longer be hidden and used for someone else's gain.

"For millennia mankind has exploited Venus' gifts, and Venus has allowed herself to be exploited because she knows that she is empty beneath that beautiful form."

Jupiter opens her mouth to defend her mother, but no words come out.

"I feel so alone whenever I come here," Venus says.

"Humanity needs you to distract it with your beauty," Dag says coolly, "but we don't."

"Enough!" Havah shouts. "Must we incessantly squabble? Unlike the rest of you, I have spent a long time intervening in the lives of men. I have learnt that humanity needs material pleasures. The gifts of the earth are to be enjoyed. The teachings of the Great Light alone are not enough for humans to survive on. They need fortune, fame, even beauty to appreciate the joys of material existence, and also its limits. Venus is the only one who can teach humanity that."

Venus sighs and gives a fake smile. She releases the phoenix feather. It lingers in the center of the Cosmic Womb. She gently parts her mouth and begins singing.

She has the voice of an angel; a poignant sound that tugs deeply at the heartstrings of everyone. Those present take their places at the Cosmic Round Table – everyone seated, everyone silent. Venus raises her arms and moves them soothingly, each movement choreographed to look natural. The phoenix feather moves higher and higher before engraving itself into the Little Light's heart.

Venus finishes her song and takes a bow. Everyone claps in appreciation. Venus slowly rises, each movement deliberate.

"It is the Great Light that blessed me with great beauty," Venus says. "I am the physical manifestation of its perfection, and my daughter Jupiter is the spiritual manifestation of its teachings. Without my existence, there would be neither poetry nor poets; neither stories nor storytellers; neither artwork nor artists; neither gems nor jewelry; neither flowers nor perfumes. I make the world beautiful so that it can be admired and loved.

"It is not my fault that mankind seeks to possess and exploit beauty. All I know is that I bring it into existence. But like all things that are born, they must one day die. It is not my fault that mankind seeks to hold onto that which must perish after its time is done. It is not my fault that mankind takes beauty and turns it into something ugly."

A heavy silence hangs in the Cosmic Womb. No fighting, no bickering. There were no words left.

"You have rejected me, Little Light," Venus says finally.

"Some of us are used to rejection," Rahu says. "Unfortunately, our beautiful Venus is not. How does it feel, to know that you don't belong, to feel that you are not wanted?"

"I feel insignificant," Venus says. "That, despite all the abundance I can give, it is not enough. There was an age where women's bodies were revered, when mankind knew that it was a woman's body that brought life into the world. That world is long gone. Even the old stories of that time no longer remain. What happened?"

"You gave birth to a son," Diana says, "with your vanity and his father's determination."

"Mars?" Venus says. "What has he got to do with this?"

"Everything," Diana says.

Dag gazes at Venus and feels his heart soften slightly. *Perhaps I have been too harsh on her. Perhaps there is more to her than meets the eye.*

Dag reaches forward and puts a hand on Venus' shoulder. Despite her great beauty, Dag has always known that Venus quietly suffers inside. "Perhaps the Little Lights yearnings and yours are one and the same."

"Perhaps," Venus says.

"It is all as it was written," Dag says finally. "It always is as it was written."

Chapter 9:

Start a Fire

The loud thud of heavy boots breaks up the tension in the room.

"If it isn't Venus' most beloved offspring," Diana says sarcastically.

Jupiter looks hurt by the remark, but remains quiet. She has always known that Mars is her mother's favorite.

"My son!" Venus says as she rushes to embrace Mars.

Mars half-heartedly hugs Venus and flicks her off.

"Mother," Mars says. "How many times have I told you to stop calling me that? I have a name."

"You will always be a little boy in my eyes."

Mars shrugs off the comment, mildly irritated. "Greetings," he says. "I see we're all here except my father. Why am I not surprised?"

"You look all scruffy," Venus sweeps forwards to straighten Mars' hair. "You really should put more effort into your appearance."

Mars raises his eyebrow and shakes his head.

"Stop touching me," Mars says.

"But I am your mother!"

Mercury looks at this open display of unnecessary affection with muted disgust, quietly thankful his mother wasn't this touchy-feely with him. *Looks like there is something worse than my father's lectures.*

"Mercury," Havah says smiling. "I can read thoughts, remember?"

Mercury grins. Mars and Mercury were playmates growing up. These days they aren't as close as they used to be, but a quiet respect remains. They are the two sons of the great fathers of the Cosmos. They are so alike, and yet so different.

"Will someone get this woman off me?" Mars says in irritation.

"This woman?" Venus barks. "How dare you speak to me in that way? I am your mother—"

"I gave you life, blah blah blah," Mars says nonchalantly. "How many times do I have to tell you that I don't care. I am not here to live out your failed dreams, or correct your quiet sufferings. I am here to carve out my own destiny."

"How can you be so selfish? How can you reject me in this way, after everything that I've given you?"

"It is you that is selfish. Stop living through me. I am not an extension of you."

Venus takes a step back. Her eyes look to the ground.

"All mothers want the best for their sons," Venus says. "It is only natural. I only wanted to see you succeed."

"Because you think that my success is your success."

"Why are you so rebellious?"

"I don't need you anymore, mother. And if you haven't noticed, I haven't needed you for a while."

"All little boys need their mother."

"I AM NOT A LITTLE BOY!"

Rahu breathes fire, unable to hold it in any longer. Rahu has always accepted Jupiter's teasing as good fun, but watching Venus and Mars is just painful. No matter how much he pushes her away, she clings on desperately. "My apologies," Rahu says once he composes himself.

"Is my sister still calling you a baby dragon?" Mars asks.

"Unfortunately so."

"What is it with the women in my family?"

"They love too much."

Mars laughs and takes his seat at the Cosmic Round Table. He is the 'baby' of his family. He grew up with the abundant love of his mother and sister, and the harsh, strict discipline of his father. As a child, he was the apple of his mother's eye, doted on and cared for like no other Celestial Being. Venus loved Jupiter too, but not in the same way.

His father Saturn grew tired of Venus' incessant coddling and sent Mars out into the world alone. Initially, Mars was scared and unsure of himself. He faced many challenges and hardships. But with time, Mars learnt to stand on his own two feet. He understood the real reason behind Saturn's tough love. Jupiter, on the other hand, has only ever known Saturn's tenderness, for it is she who was chosen by the Great Light itself.

"Brother," Jupiter says. "It's good to see you."

"It's good to see you, too."

The two siblings share an awkward hug. They were never close, not even as children. Venus' overbearing love for Mars, and her unvoiced jealousy over her own daughter's great gifts, had never left room for any deep bond to develop between the two siblings.

"You grow wiser with the passing of time," Mars says quietly admiring Jupiter as he would an old friend.

"And you grow more resilient," Jupiter says. "I'm proud of you and all that you've achieved on your own."

"Thank you, sister."

"How come I don't have a sibling?" Mercury asks with a pout.

Diana laughs. She knows how the only child always secretly longs for a sibling.

"There was no way I could have watched over you and the earth," Diana says. "And you were already quite the handful, mind you."

Mercury nods and accedes to the fact. He knows his mother had a lot of other responsibilities outside of him, unlike Venus. He is quietly glad his mother had, and still has, her own life. Venus' coddling is unbearable to watch. It is one thing to live your life in your father's shadow, and another thing altogether to live under your mother's thumb.

"Mars," Dag says, "you have grown up to be a fine young man."

Mars turns to face Dag and bows his head slightly, humbled by the comment, for he knows that Dag is not one for sugary words.

Mars is dressed impeccably in an army suit. His red hair is immaculately groomed, his face is clean-shaven, and his green eyes shine with a youthful innocence despite all the horrors they have seen since he'd left home. His body is marked with scars that have healed over. Mars looks strong, determined, and resolute. Definitely not the type of person that anyone would need to coddle.

"Mars, I have a present for you," Rahu says.

"Oh?" Mars says. "And what might that be?"

"A Little Light with a North Node in Aries."

Mars grins. The constellation of Aries is one of his own constellations.

"A North Node in Aries means…," Mars says. "A South Node in Libra…"

"Indeed."

Libra is one of Venus' constellations. The Little Light has spent many incarnations blessed by Venus, and is now assigned a new life task – to embody the Arian energy of Mars.

"Hello, Little Light," Mars says. "I'm your destiny."

The Little Light looks at Mars with a tinge of disgust.

"You are Mangal," the Little Light says. "I remember you. You were but a spoilt little boy the last time we met. You incessantly threw tantrums and picked fights with everyone. You were a selfish brat."

Mars winces, but keeps his facial expression stoic. Of course, he remembers those days. His mother had always put his needs first. No matter what mischief he got up to, he could do no wrong in his mother's eyes. He played many pranks on the other Celestial Beings, even wreaked havoc on the Little Lights under his care. Whenever Mars looks back on those days, he is filled with a mixture of shame and remorse.

"Mars is no longer the naughty boy he once was," Dag says. "He is now a man we are all deeply proud of."

Mars bows his head again in Dag's direction.

"Little Light," Mars says. "I had so much to learn back then. I thought that being a man meant putting yourself first and bullying others into following you, no matter what the cost. Now I understand that being a man means taking responsibility, and taking charge as a leader, so that others will follow you of their own volition."

The Little Light observes Mars quizzically. There is something about him that reminds her of herself.

"Despite your outward appearance of strength," the Little Light says. "I sense something deeply vulnerable about you."

Mars is taken aback by the Little Light's remark, but manages to keep his outward demeanor stoic. Very few can discern the vulnerable side of his nature.

"It is not easy to be a warrior," Diana says. "Life can be lonely when you have no one to share it with. Mars has lived alone his whole life, with no one by his side. There is a part of him that longs for a companion."

"But he's always had me," Venus says. "I was always there for him."

"It was not a relationship between equals," Diana says. "You are his mother."

"Mars doesn't need any other woman," Venus insists.

"Mother," Mars says clasping his hands together. "You do not know what my needs are. And you most certainly do not know what is best for me."

"Together we could have—" Venus says.

"We've talked about this, mother. You live your life, and I live mine."

"Ungrateful child! Now that you are all grown up, you don't want me anymore."

Mars shrugs. It's pointless to argue, for no matter how much he fights with his mother there's no winning. From the day he was born, he's had to contend with Venus' possessiveness. She treats him as she would one of her most expensive jewels – to be adored, gazed at, loved, and cherished. If his father Saturn hadn't stepped in and pushed him to find his own path, he would still be under his mother's thumb.

"The Arian path is one of courage," Rahu says. "Of bravery and fearlessness. You see, Little Light, it is not that Mars doesn't feel afraid, it is that he doesn't let his fear stop him from doing what he wants to do, and what he needs to do.

"He knew that he would incur his mother's disappointment by forging his own path, but he did it anyway. In the process, he might have lost the close bond he had with his mother, but he has gained our respect. More importantly, he has gained his own self-respect, and that is something no one can ever take away from him."

The Little Light turns around and walks towards Mars, who quickly gets up from his seat at the Cosmic Round Table. The Little Light and Mars observe each other closely, like old friends meeting after a long time.

"There is something of my old yearnings in you, Little Light," Mars says.

The Little Light nods. She puts her hand in his. Mars is taken aback by this unusual display of warmth. It has been a long time since he felt such tenderness. The Little Light runs her other hand through his hair. Mars momentarily shuts his eyes, taking in the moment as the Little Light's essence reverberates through him.

"Despite all that you have achieved," the Little Light says, "you are so incredibly lonely."

"Everything in this world has its price, Little Light," Mars says. "When you rejected Venus, you rejected companionship and partnership."

The Little Light leans forward and embraces Mars.

Mars gives away a small and rare genuine smile. He is no stranger to the adoration of women, but this is innocent and far more primal; two of the Great Light's creations holding each other as kin.

"You must accept your twin," Mars says gently in the Little Light's ear. "I promise you that with my blessing, it will be a union of two souls who have earned each other, and who will spend their days as equals."

The Little Light lets go and looks Mars in the eye. Unlike the others, there is an innocence and simplicity about Mars that she trusts.

"I'm scared," the Little Light says, "that things will be as they were in previous incarnations."

"I will not let that happen," Rahu says. "You are born with a North Node in Aries. I will not allow you to be number two in anyone's life. You will live your life on your terms and when the time is right, you will attract a twin who will respect you for who you are."

"Do you have a twin?" the Little Light asks Mars.

"We all have a twin," Mars says.

The Little Light nods.

"I like you, Mars," the Little Light says.

Mars smiles. Unlike his mother, he smiles from the heart.

"I like you too, Little Light," Mars says.

"I accept my twin," the Little Light says.

♂

"Mother," Mars says. "You know what you need to do."

"Until now," Venus says, "the Celestial Beings have given. But to accept your twin, I will need something from you."

"And what's that?" the Little Light asks.

"A little spark from your soul," Venus says.

"Why?"

"It will bind your soul with his in a shared destiny."

The Little Light tilts her head and takes a step back.

"You still do not trust me," Venus says, exasperated.

"It is not that… What if I get the wrong twin?"

Venus nods, fully understanding the Little Light's concerns.

"You were wise to choose Venus in Capricorn, Little Light," Venus says. "You will not surrender your soul to someone unworthy. You can, and might even have many lovers, but there can only be one twin."

"How will I know he's my twin?"

"He will manifest in your life when the time is right."

"How will I know that I won't end up with the wrong person?"

"Because it is the Lore," Dag says with certainty.

The Little Light nods.

"Are you ready?" Venus asks.

"I am."

"Jupiter," Venus says. "You know what you need to do."

Jupiter takes a deep breath and puts her hand on her heart. "By the power vested in me by the Great Light," she says, "I humbly request a spark from Liora's soul."

A small shimmering blue spark emerges from inside the Little Light's heart. Jupiter removes a pomegranate from her cloak. She gently opens the fruit. Within it are other little blue sparks, the remnants of other Little Lights who have willingly surrendered a little bit of themselves. The Little Light's blue spark hangs in the room before settling inside the fruit.

Jupiter closes the pomegranate. "You have chosen wisely, Little Light," Jupiter says. "Now there is another matter. You will also need to accept Venus."

"Why?" the Little Light asks.

"For it is she, who gives a woman her physical form. Without her, your soul won't have a physical body. It is why you are still in lucid form."

"With all the grief she has caused…"

"Little Light," Rahu interjects. "You were born with a Ketu in Libra – one of Venus' constellations. Venus is your shadow, but she is also your karma. When you achieve the heights of Aries, you will long for its opposite. It is the way the universe is designed. Everything works on a polarity, on an axis.

"As you have seen for yourself, Mars has achieved great heights, but he is lonely. He now understands that dharma can only take him so far. He must redeem the gifts from his shadow if he is truly to ascend."

The Little Light crinkles her eyebrows. "Redeem the gifts of his shadow?" she asks.

"Take my hand," Mars says.

The Little Light puts her hand in Mars'. A vision seizes her.

Maya, a voice whispers. Maya. She sees the silhouette of a man but she cannot see his face. You did it, Maya. I'm so proud of you. I know it hasn't been easy. I know what you had to go through to get here. But this is your moment now. Go forth and claim what's rightfully yours. You've earned it.

Maya gets up from a chair. The thundering applause of a faceless crowd greets her as she walks to the podium alone. All these people, here for me? They do not know who I really am. They only know me for my work and all I've achieved. A vague sense of panic sets in.

She looks into the crowd and makes out the silhouette of the man she saw earlier. He's smiling, tears of pride streaming down his face.

The Little Light lets go of Mars' hand and shakes him off.

"What was that?" the Little Light asks. "Who was that? Why couldn't I see his face?"

"What you saw was not a prophecy," Pirouzeh says, "but a possibility, which is why it was so vague. When you achieve the heights of Rahu, you must remember to unlock the gifts of Ketu."

"I don't understand."

"You are not meant to. Not right now anyway. That is what your life's journey is meant to teach you. But for now, know that you must accept Venus. You can no longer reject her."

The Little Light's hair morphs into a deep dark red. "I will not."

"That is your choice," Pirouzeh says proudly. "Free will is – for better or for worse – embedded in the Universe's design."

"So...Mars," Jupiter chimes in before Venus has a chance to speak. "What constellation are you in?"

"Taurus."

"Oh! One of mummy's constellations! A wise choice, Little Light – slow to anger, but when you do, your enemies better watch out!"

"The silent hidden strength," Mars says. "The slow and steady tortoise that outwits the hare and wins the race."

"What tortoise? What hare? What race?" Jupiter asks. "Life is about the journey, about the splendor of living in the moment, about the happiness that ensues from the sheer joy of being alive."

Mars smacks himself on the head. His sister's optimism has no boundaries.

"Isn't that right, baby Rahu?" Jupiter quips.

Rahu breathes fire in her direction.

Dag laughs. At the end of the day, it is as it was written. It always is as it was written.

Chapter 10:

Don't Give Up

Unlike the others, he walks without ceremony. No big entrance. No grand display. His appearance is austere, minimalist, and dignified. He wears a clean black suit with a silvery-blue shirt and tie. His hands are in his pockets. All the Celestial Beings turn around and look at him, expressions of fear and respect etched across their faces. They bow their heads slightly as a mark of respect. The mood always turns eerily somber whenever he walks into the Cosmic Womb.

Silence and stillness. It scares the other Celestial Beings. But not him.

Unbothered by the undivided attention, he only focuses on the task at hand: walking to the Cosmic Round Table. Each footstep, slow and deliberate. He is tall with striking dark and silver hair - each silver strand a hard-earned and venerable display of the wisdom that can only come with time and experience.

"Greetings, Surya, Great Father of the Universe," he says.

His voice is matter of fact. Deep. Low. Cold. Distant. No avarice. No happiness. No pretenses. It just is.

"Greetings, Saturn," the Sun says respectfully. "The Great Father of Time."

Saturn bows ninety degrees, and the Sun follows suit.

The Sun was created by the Great Light to be the Father of the Universe. Saturn, on the other hand, had to earn his place. He was the Solar System's very first planet. As a child, he was gangly, awkward, and tedious to teach. Saturn was a man of few words, slow to learn anything new, and resistant to change. But now he is the Sun's equal - the de facto co-ruler of the Solar System.

"Greetings, Great Mother of the Cosmos," Saturn says with a slight heaviness in his voice.

He is so unlike any of us, Diana thinks as she turns to look at him. Saturn was born during the eclipse, when Rahu swallowed the Sun and the world was enveloped in shadows. If the Sun was born of pure light, then Saturn was born of pure darkness.

"Shani," Diana says, addressing him by his Vedic name. "I am so proud of you. You did well for yourself."

Saturn bows slightly, an unshed tear in his eye; a man of few words and even fewer public displays of affection. He is not a man to wear his heart on his sleeve. Especially in front of the two luminaries - the Celestial Beings who abandoned him and, as a consequence, hurt him beyond recognition.

"May we speak in private?" the Sun asks.

"Yes, the three of us," Diana says.

Saturn locks his blue eyes on both of them and blinks stoically. He takes a deep breath, slowly contemplating the thought. His expressionless face hides his true sentiments.

"We can discuss any business we have in front of the others," he says finally.

"Saturn," the Sun implores.

"It's too late. You had your time. You all had your time, and that is all you can get. It is the Lore."

Once Saturn's mind is made up, there is no shaking him. Unlike Mercury, who lacks focus and remains flexible, Saturn is immovable, and resolute.

"I deserve your respect," the Sun says.

"Is that so?" Saturn says coldly. "And exactly what have you done to earn it?"

"I am the Sun. The Father of the Cosmos."

"The Great Light gifted you with everything so that you may give everything. I respect the Great Light: the Source of All Creation. You, on the other hand...beyond common decency, I owe you nothing."

"You orbit around me, not the other way around. It will do you well to remember that!"

"There is no denying the fact. This argument is finished."

"This argument isn't finished till I say it's finished."

Saturn rolls his eyes and turns away from the Sun. He knows arguing with the Sun is futile, but if he kept silent, the others would have mistaken it for weakness.

"Husband," Venus says, with a huge genuine smile. "I'm so happy to see you."

She runs around the table and hugs him. Saturn's eyes soften and wrinkle, giving away a secret smile. Venus has a way of bringing out the best in him. Around her, he is slightly less guarded, slightly more human.

"Hello, Venus," he says as he pulls away. "The pleasure is all mine."

Saturn holds Venus' hands in his and takes a good look at her. Saturn notices every little detail. His slow inspecting gaze may make many feel uncomfortable, but not Venus. She adores Saturn. He makes her feel safe, treasured, and accepted for who she is; not what she can give.

"You grow more and more beautiful with time," Saturn says as he gives his wife a kiss on the forehead. "And you dazzle even the coldest of hearts with your grace and your charm."

Venus smiles and beams with pride. To her, Saturn has always been that protective duty-prone husband every woman should have. He was always there for her, no matter what.

Mercury looks at the two of them with a tinge of disgust. Mercury's never been one for open displays of affection. *Get a room.*

"Father Saturn," Mercury says taking on a cool and serious demeanor, "Greetings."

"Greetings to you, too. How's business, Mercury?"

"Could be better, but I can't complain."

"I see you are the ascendant...It is a wise choice for this day and age."

"That's what I was telling the others, but they wouldn't believe me."

"Don't hold it against them. They have their heads in the clouds."

"Well said, Father Time," Dag says. "Some are born with great destinies, others create their own. It is only you and your son Mars that have had to forge their own path in the Cosmos."

Saturn looks over at Mars. *Ahh... He's grown up nicely. A man of the world.* Saturn walks towards Mars and gives him a pat on the back. They do not exchange words, but they understand each other well enough not to. Unlike the Sun,

Saturn has never been the type of man to give the same long sermons over and over again.

Saturn teaches by setting a good example and expecting others to emulate him. He knows that he cannot expect his children to do what he does not. Whilst he loves his wife Venus, he has always disagreed with her coddling. All that overindulgence is enjoyable, but ultimately worthless unless tempered with tough love. The world needs structure, boundaries and discipline, or else chaos will reign.

"The Little Light has rejected Venus," Havah says.

"I am aware," Saturn says.

"But you know that only Venus can give the Little Light a human body."

"I am aware."

"Daddy," Jupiter's happy voice chirps in.

She reaches for her father and hugs him. Jupiter gives him a big kiss on the cheek before she rests her head on his shoulder. Saturn laughs in a rare display of warmth. Jupiter is the only one who can bring out his suppressed gentleness.

"Beloved daughter," Saturn says. "You are the best thing that ever happened to me."

Venus is rebuffed by that remark. After Jupiter was born, Venus had no choice but to shrink into the background. Jupiter is loved and adored by everyone; friend and foe alike. Venus knows this jealousy is unbecoming of her, but she can't help herself. All the other Celestial Beings know that Venus is deeply envious of her own daughter, but they have never given voice to the sentiment.

"I wish everyone was lucky enough to have a father like you," Jupiter says.

Mars smiles. He has never known his father's affection the way Jupiter did. But unlike Venus, Mars holds no remorse in his heart. He knows that Saturn did what was best for Mars in the long haul. Mars remembers a time when he didn't always feel this way.

"I hate you!" Mars yells.

"That is your choice," Saturn responds coldly.

"How can you send your only son away from home? Look at the Sun, look at how he guides Mercury every step of the way, grooming him, watching over him."

"Mercury will forever be under his father's shadow. I don't want you to live your life under your mother's. One day you will understand. Now leave! Create your own destiny. Fulfil your own dharma."

"I hate you, father. I hate you. I never want to see you again. I will never return to your abode for as long as I live."

"That is your choice."

Mars shakes his head as he remembers the argument. Arian energy at its worst – hot-headed, impulsive and childish. Experience has tempered the heat in his soul with a certain steadiness and sturdiness he wasn't born with. He has tamed the fire that once burned inside him and destroyed everything in its path. These days the only person that can fire him up is his mother...

"I see the Little Light has chosen a North Node in Aries," Saturn says, addressing Mars. "A wise choice."

"I will do my very best," Mars says, "to guide this soul to fulfil its mission."

"I know, my son. I have full faith in you. The Great Light has honored both you and me with this great task. For this is no ordinary soul."

Saturn peers at the Little Light, sensing the desire and deep yearning that reside within her. Like Ketu, Saturn can tap into the energy stream of the soul from previous incarnations. But unlike Ketu, who causes great suffering to bring forth spiritual liberation, Saturn works in a pragmatic way: by placing the structures, boundaries, and burdens necessary for the soul in its human existence.

"Little Light," Saturn says, "we have awaited your arrival for a long time."

"Me?" the Little Light says. "I am just a Little Light, no different from the other Little Lights out there."

Saturn raises his eyebrows, momentarily taken aback by this remark for he knows that this is no ordinary Little Light.

"You underestimate yourself," Saturn says. "You fear the tremendous power you possess. That has been your undoing in previous incarnations. You think every soul is capable of reaching great heights. That every soul has the same capacity you do. You gave your light away in previous incarnations so others could shine while you stood in the shadows. This made those around you stronger, while your own light diminished with each moment.

"And yet, your light is so strong that even the Celestial Beings are awed by it. You are Liora, the Chosen Light of the Great Light."

"Liora?" the Little Light asks. "What does this all mean? The others called me that, too."

Saturn looks at Dag, then Havah, and then at Dag again.

"You have rejected Venus' gifts," Saturn says. "May I ask why?"

"I experienced great suffering in my previous incarnations because of her. Because of her 'gifts'. And it was all a sham."

"Her gifts may well have been a sham, but that is not the real reason why you've rejected her."

The Little Light looks at Saturn in shock and takes a step back.

"You're afraid," Saturn says. "Very afraid. To leave the Great Light and the Cosmic Womb… this eternal place of infinite light and wonder… for a world that you know is filled with suffering and strife. But leave, you must. It is the Lore."

Saturn examines the Little Light with a stoic expression. The Cosmic Womb is silent. In front of Saturn, no Celestial Being would dare to have an argument or make a scene. The Little Light takes two steps back in a futile attempt to put some space between her and Saturn.

"Do not fear me, child, I am merely a messenger," Saturn says. "I understand your fears, and I am here to tell you they are perfectly normal."

Saturn turns away from the Little Light to give her a moment. Saturn's eyes meet Mercury's. A knowing glance passes between them. *My little brother – the open secret everyone knows but nobody dares to mention. Perhaps that is best. The age gap between us is so big that I am more like a father than a brother. Besides, my family never cared much for me, nor I for them.*

Saturn's eyes meet his mother's. She wasn't Diana when he was born. He was conceived when the Moon was in Capricorn, not Aries. It still amazes him that his mother can change her physical form every two and a half days. Not that he ever knew her love. He once grieved for the loss, but now he no longer gives it much thought. Besides, he has Venus and Jupiter to give him all the joy that only women can bring.

Saturn is about to look at the Sun, but he changes his mind... *Not in the mood for another one of his sermons. I would rather spend the rest of my life at the edge of the Cosmos in solitary confinement than have to hear his irritating voice bellowing through the Cosmic Womb.*

Finally, Saturn glances at Rahu and Ketu, his natural allies and friends. Unlike the other Celestial Beings, humans need Rahu and Ketu as much as the lunar nodes need them. They bring the twin forces of karma and dharma to the world, giving meaning and purpose to the human experience. Without them, mankind's existence would represent a cyclical monotonous dance of the cosmos with no free will.

After observing his fellow Celestial Beings, Saturn returns his gaze to the Little Light.

"My child," Saturn says. "Life is a great gift. You are blessed to receive it. Despite all the trials, tribulations, and adversaries; you know deep down that the human experience is truly worth living."

"They told me," the Little Light says, "that I will suffer greatly till I turn 31. That life will resemble a long dark tunnel with no end in sight."

"Perhaps that is true, but beautiful gems can emerge from dirt. Struggle can teach you self-discipline and resilience. Opulence and decadence can never do that. I have some gifts for you, my child. Would you like to know what they are?"

The Little Light gazes at Saturn with a mixture of respect and curiosity. She walks over to Saturn and sits down next to him. She intuitively trusts him, as a child would a father.

"Do you accept my gifts?" Saturn asks.

"I do."

"You are born with a Saturn in Sagittarius: one of my daughter's very own constellations. I believe Jupiter has already promised you safe passage through life's darkest days?"

The Little Light remembers how Jupiter had ordered all the Celestial Beings to watch over her so that no great harm would come to her.

"She did," the Little Light says.

Saturn gently places a hand on the Little Light's shoulder.

"You see, my child," Saturn says. "I did not send Mars away from home into a cold dark world to fend for himself because I did not love him. I sent him out there because I knew he could do it. He had it in him all along. You too have it in you to survive life's hard tests, so that you may grow strong and resilient.

"Unlike beauty and loveliness that fade with the passing of time, nothing and no one can ever take our wisdom and inner strength away from us. It teaches us to bear the hard times with dignity, and enjoy the good times knowing we've earned them.

"Can you understand?"

The Little Light puts her hand in Saturn's. The Celestial Beings are surprised by the gesture. Saturn has never been the touchy-feely type.

Dag notices a certain likeness between the two of them; a quiet strength and determination to push forward.

"I understand," the Little Light says.

"I will gift you with great teachers who will come to your aid to guide you," Saturn says. "The lessons they have to teach you will not be easy. Some of these teachers will be kind and benevolent. Others will be cruel and demanding. Some will come in the guise of lovers. Others, in the form of kin. You might even meet some friends that turn out to be foes and vice versa. But they are all there to teach you so you can learn what you need to ascend.

"You will have a lot to learn from your elders, for one day, you will be an elder yourself. Your elders will pass down their teachings to you, and the day will come when you'll have to do the same for the next generation."

Saturn reaches into his pocket and removes a gold necklace with a pendant in the shape of a candle flame.

"I gift you with this," Saturn says. "For gold never rusts. I promise you that the wisdom you acquire through the first 31 years of your human life will never fade. It will prepare you for what is to come. When you put on this pendant, you accept both Venus' gifts and mine. For it is I who made the gold, but it is she who made it beautiful. Together, we create beautiful things built to last."

The Little Light looks at the candle-flame-shaped gold pendant. She remembers the Great Light, and how she was but a tiny figment emanating from it. She remembers how she chose her soul task. There were so many she could have chosen from, but this is the one that called out to her.

The Little Light unhooks the pendant and puts it on. Her astral body begins to solidify. Her long dark wavy hair stretches to her waist. Her skin changes to a shade of cara-mel. Her eyes sparkle like golden ambers. Her nose grows tall, regal, and proud. Her body morphs into the shape of an adult woman.

"Wow," Mercury says, looking pleased. "You're beautiful."

"Indeed," Diana says. "There is still a little something Venusian about you, but it is hidden. I look at you, and I see Jupiter, with a touch of Saturn."

"Erm… hello?" Mercury says. "I'm the Lagna Lord. I'm the one that…"

"Ahem…" Saturn says, clearing his throat. "You sound rather familiar… Like someone we all know."

Everyone in the Cosmic Womb laughs.

"Like father, like son," the Sun says. "He really does take after me. He is rather intelligent, quick-thinking…"

"Oh dear Lord," Pirouzeh says, chiming in. "Do you ever just shut up?"

"You dis…dis..disgraceful owl!"

Pirouzeh's hoots reverberate through the Cosmic Womb along with everyone else's laughs.

ħ

When everyone calms down, Havah and Dag look at each other and give a quick nod.

"The moment of birth is drawing close," Dag says. "Everyone, please take your places."

The Celestial Beings quickly shuffle around and take their seats at the Cosmic Round Table. Ketu sits in the fourth house. Saturn places himself in the seventh and his wife Venus sits in the eighth house next to him. The Sun and Mercury take the ninth, much to Mercury's unveiled irritation. The Moon, Jupiter, and Rahu form a conjunction in the tenth house; whilst Mars winds up in the eleventh.

"What does this all mean?" the Little Light asks.

"If we told you everything," Mars says, "life would lose its sense of adventure."

The Little Light smiles.

"The houses," Mercury interjects, "represent the areas of your life where you will expend the planetary energy you are born with. As all the Celestial Beings – except Ketu – are in the seventh to eleventh houses – much of your life's energy will be spent contributing to the collective destiny of mankind."

"Will I remember all this once I am born?" the Little Light asks.

"Perhaps," Mercury says sadly.

"Will we meet again?"

"Perhaps."

"I feel like you're all my friends."

"We are your friends, Little Light," Jupiter says. "If you ever need us, all you have to do is look up at the night sky and we will be there."

"Promise?"

"Promise."

Chapter 11:

Long Nights

"**N**ow that we are all here," Dag says. "Havah and I have an announcement to make."

Saturn turns to Dag and gives a slight nod. Mercury smiles proudly, but remains silent. The Celestial Beings vaguely know what Dag is about to say, but the Little Light remains unaware.

"Dear Celestial Beings," Dag continues. "As you all are aware, we have in our presence, Liora – the Chosen Light of the Great Light. It has been many millennia since a desire this strong has manifested in the world, and it is with good reason.

"You see, Havah and I have grown tired. We are old, and ready to let go. Unlike the rest of you, Havah and I were human once. We were granted immortality by the Great Light so that we may watch over humanity and intervene in their affairs if necessary. But a new age is dawning. An age that will require a new beginning.

"The old must make way for the new.

"Liora – or Maya – as she will be known in her next human incarnation, is the next Mother Guardian of the Lore."

The Celestial Beings take a deep breath in and out. They had all known, but did not speak of it, for it is against the Lore to reveal a Little Light's destiny before it has fully accepted its soul mission.

"What?" the Little Light says. "Does that mean that you will die?"

"No, Little Light," Havah says. "Dag and I are immortal, so we cannot die. We will receive a new soul mission once we have passed the baton to you."

"Does that I mean that I will become immortal too?"

"Perhaps. We do not know the entire cosmic design. Besides, free will still exists."

"But what does it mean? To be the Mother Guardian of the Lore? Or shall I say the new Mother Guardian of the Lore…"

"You will discover that through the course of your life. Dag and I will watch over you and guide you along your path."

"What if I fail?"

"At the end of the day," Dag says. "It always is as it was written."

"But if I'm the future Mother Guardian," the Little Light says, "then that means that…"

"There is a Father Guardian," Dag says finishing the sentence. "Yes, Little Light, the feminine and masculine principles have always existed in equilibrium in the Grand Design."

"Who is he?" the Little Light asks.

"We do not know, yet."

"What do you mean?"

"There are a few possibilities. You have accepted this life task of your own free will. The Father Guardian will have to do the same. With one caveat…"

"And that is?"

"The Mother Guardian of the Lore is blessed and watched over by Jupiter herself, the Great Guru of the Cosmos. The Father Guardian, on the other hand, is watched over by Saturn, the Great Taskmaster. He will have to earn his place there."

"Earn his place?"

"Indeed, Little Light. The Mother Guardian creates, destroys, and maintains order by controlling the cycle of life and death. The Father Guardian has to work with free will to manipulate probabilities and create coincidences. He has to make sure that free will doesn't interfere too much in the Grand Design. He cannot do that if he does not earn his place."

"How will I know when I have met someone worthy?"

"That is my job," Saturn says.

Dag and Havah exchange a glance. They know how quickly Saturn can turn things upside down and break things up in a partnership that is not strong enough to withstand life's toughest tests. Dag remembers all the trials that Saturn put him through before he became the Father Guardian of the Lore — but then again, if he had not gone through those tough years, he would not be the man he is today.

"You trust me don't you, Little Light?" Saturn asks.

"I do."

"Then don't worry your weary heart."

The Little Light nods.

"Now you must go," Saturn says.

"Am I about to be born?" the Little Light asks.

"Yes," Dag says. "But first, you must die."

"What?"

"It is time," Saturn says.

Saturn, the Cosmic Father of Time, spins the Cosmic Round Table. The Little Light, Havah, and Dag vanish. The Celestial Beings remain in the Cosmic Womb.

"I really did like her," Mercury says with a touch of melancholy. "Till next time, Little Light."

∞

"What just happened?" the Little Light asks. "Where are we?"

"At your funeral," Dag says. "You see, Little Light, life and death are two sides of the same coin."

"Why am I here?"

"It is the Lore. The funeral rites represent both the ending and the beginning. No matter what life we lived, in death, we are all equals. In death, all is revealed."

An open casket lays solitary in a funeral parlor. The body has been washed and the orifices are stuffed with cotton.

"Is that me?" the Little Light asks.

"In a sense," Dag says.

"What do you mean?"

"That was the body your soul inhabited in your previous life. As you are now dead, the body has no life force. So in a way, it is not you anymore."

"I was a woman in my last life, too."

"Indeed. Your previous incarnation took place in a different era than the one you'll be born into."

"The Cosmic Womb... You said it was a vortex before time comes into existence. If my body's been here the whole time, then how was I there?"

"The Cosmic Womb is a realm that exists outside human notions of time and place. Think of it as a vortex of eternal time, where the past, present, and future flow in a continuous stream."

The Little Light stares down at the coffin. Her old body is dressed in a white robe made of silk. Her face shows traces of makeup – the final embalming rites. Her hair is white and neatly wrapped in a bun. Her skin looks waxy and cold. Six coins with a hole in the middle are tied with a string that is wrapped around her hand.

"What are the coins for?" the Little Light asks.

"Gifts from your descendants for the journey in the afterlife."

"The afterlife?"

"Well...each culture has its own ideas about what happens after death."

"Will I be born into the same culture in my next life?"

"Cultures change with the generations. Nothing lasts forever. It is the Lore."

The Little Light notices a white wolf sitting by the casket. Something about it seems familiar...

"What's that?" the Little Light asks.

"Your spirit animal in your last life," Dag says. "It is not the spirit animal you were born with, but the one you received when you turned 31 in your previous incarnation.

The wolf is both a pack animal and a solitary creature. It is also a leader that trusts its instinct. Do you remember its name? If you do, you may call out to it and it will answer."

The Little Light takes a moment to think. Her memories are fuzzy. They reside somewhere inside her, and yet are not accessible. Even looking down at her own dead body feels far away. There appears to be no connection between what happened in the Cosmic Womb and the scene unfolding in front of her.

The wolf suddenly turns in her direction. Its yellow eyes peer into hers. She's trying to recognize it, but is unable to. The wolf howls. The sound is unbearably tragic and mournful. The Little Light puts her hands to her ears, but the howl sounds like its reverberating from inside her.

"I cannot bear… it," the Little Light says.

"Unlike owls that are independent by nature," Dag says, "the wolf is an enduringly loyal creature that does not like to be separated from its pack for extended periods of time."

The wolf continues howling, its cries desolate and pitiable; a sound of pure suffering that begs to be heard and answered. "How can an animal so proud be so woeful?" the Little Light asks.

"You were the matriarch of the Wolf Clan," Dag says. "Your passing is a source of great sorrow to both human and spirit animal alike."

"I still can't remember its name…"

"You must concentrate!"

The Little Light digs deep, trying to access the memories of her previous incarnation, but nothing comes to mind. The scenes before her eyes are blurry, incoherent and vague – as if they were someone else's life she was watching from far away, like an unwelcome voyeur.

"Mistress," a voice suddenly whispers clearly. "I pledge my loyalty to you till death."

"I remember," the Little Light says. "His name is Okami."

Okami turns to look at Dag and the Little Light. The wolf can see them now.

"Mistress," the wolf says. "I was worried you wouldn't remember me."

"I do," the Little Light says, "but barely."

"Perhaps that is for the best," Okami says. "Dag, my greetings to you."

"Pleasure to see you again, Okami."

"Mistress," the wolf says. "It was my pleasure to have served this family all these years."

"I am afraid I do not know what you speak of."

"It will come back to you. Time in the Cosmic Womb has a way of making human memories… fuzzy. But once your loved ones begin arriving, you will remember."

"Will we meet again in the next life?"

"I'm afraid not. Our work together is done. When you are gone, I will pass on."

"How come?"

"Wolves do not survive the death of their charges. It is the Lore."

"I'm sad to hear that."

"Don't be. I chose this soul task the same way you chose yours. Have you met your new spirit animal?"

"It is Pirouzeh of the Owl Clan."

"Ah… A wise choice for a soul that longs for its independence and autonomy. Can't say I'm surprised. You spent your last incarnation taking care of your pack. I suppose the time has come for you to pursue your own path, away from the incessant demands of your family and lovers."

"Lovers?"

"Yes, you had many lovers, but only one great secret affair. And of course, the jealousy of other womenfolk. I don't think life ever gave you the privilege of solitude."

A man walks into the room. He is tall with a head of curly hair. A black cord emerges between the Little Light and the man. Little Light's whole being trembles with indignant rage and anger. Old memories of fear, shame and abandonment rise up within her. *I want him dead.*

"Your first husband," Okami says. "A rich man from a wealthy family who gambled away the family fortune after his father passed away. He pursued you, captivated by your innocence and warmth, and then slowly destroyed it bit by bit. Before you married, he was a gentleman, caught up in the thrill of the chase. After marriage, he was a violent, mean, and angry drunk. Every night was a living nightmare. Thankfully you had no children together."

"Forgive me," the man whispers as he stares at the corpse. "Forgive me."

Pain sears through The Little Light. Although she is dead, the bond between them lingers. *I wish he were dead.*

"Cut the cord," Dag says.

The Little Light twitches and quivers. She cannot remember the memories, but the imprint of those old terrors remains. *How can he live so peacefully after all the suffering he caused me?*

"Cut the cord," Dag says again.

Okami growls and darts through the room, sinking its sharp teeth into the black cord, severing it forever. The Little Light whimpers in pain.

"What was that?" the Little Light asks.

"Deep-seated anger at the indignation," Dag says. "Trauma can tie two people together long after they part."

The man sinks to his knees and begins crying.

"You have no business being here," another man's voice says sternly.

The second man has a head full of silky black hair. His posture is resolute, strong, and authoritative. The first man quickly darts out of the room, tears still in his eyes.

"Your second husband," Okami says. "He married you against his mother's wishes. Like your first husband, he was captivated by your charms and your beauty. He loved you, but you never loved him. It was a marriage of convenience, a way out of your misery. He accepted you and gave you the stability and structure you never had in your first marriage, but there was no love and no passion between the two of you. He was born into poverty so he worked hard to provide for you and the family.

"His mother was cold and cruel and gave you a hard time. She was jealous of the love her son had for you. She undermined you at every turn. She tried to sabotage your relationship many times. You wanted to leave him, but felt bound by social norms, so you learnt to bear your pain alone. Things got better after his mother died. Together you have two children – a girl and a boy. He rarely saw them. You raised them alone."

A silver cord emerges between the Little Light and the second man. There is a knot in the middle of the cord.

"He feels like such a stranger," the Little Light says.

"In a sense, he was," Okami says. "You never shared your joys or pains together, only your lives."

The Little Light feels a cold hollow feeling in her heart. Unlike the first man, where the pain was unbearable, this is frosty and vacant; a space of pure emptiness.

"This cord cannot be severed," Dag says. "There is some karmic give and take left between the two of you."

"What does that mean?" the Little Light asks.

"You will meet him again in your next life," Dag says. "You will spend a few years together, but you will not be married, nor have any children. In his next life, he will be born into a family of great wealth so that he can pursue his new soul task – to learn how to love and share true intimacy.

"It will take him several lifetimes to achieve his soul task. You will grow tired of waiting for him to love you the way you need to be loved. When you finally tell him the truth, he will be unable to face it. You will leave him – the way you always wanted to in this life, but couldn't. He will go down a path of self-destruction before he finds his way again. By that time, you will be long gone down a different road."

"How do you know all this?"

"It is as it was written."

The Little Light looks at the strange man that was her husband in her last life. Did she ever know him at all?

He takes an orange rose and places it in the casket. "In the next life," he whispers.

A third man walks into the room. He is the tallest of the three men. His long hair stretches to his waist. A brief moment of guilt appears in his eyes before it is gone.

"Come to pay your last respects?" the second man asks.

The third man nods.

"I'll give you a moment," the second man says and exits the room.

The third man stares at the body. A red cord emerges between him and the Little Light. Her body fills with secret longings, fantasies, and the strong memory of a forbidden love. A vision seizes her.

He runs his hand through her hair as his other hand touches her lips. His touch is tender, warm, and full of desire. He leans forward to kiss her.

"I love you," he says.

She looks into his eyes, slightly startled. "I love you, too," she replies.

"You can always leave him."

"You know I cannot. What about the children? Besides, you are married, too."

He nods.

The vision disappears.

"Ahh…" Okami says, unsurprised. "You remember him vividly. How could you forget? You couldn't even if you wanted to."

The third man bends down and kisses the corpse on the forehead. He removes an owl's feather from his jacket pocket and places it in her right hand.

He looks up to where the Little Light is.

"You are still here," he says. "I can feel your presence. You have not crossed over yet. I know that there is a cord that still ties us together. Perhaps your memories are blurry and you are wondering how I know all of this. I am a seer – one of the greatest of my time. In your next life, you will be the Mother Guardian of the Lore. I have foreseen it.

"I gift you with this feather, with the hopes that you will have the opportunity to share your wisdom with the world. I know we will meet again in the next life. We will be married, but we will part ways, for I will be assigned another soul task. Thank you, truly. My world was a better place for having you in it. I will cherish every memory in this life and the next. Till next time, my love."

The third man walks out of the room. The Little Light's heart fills with an indescribable longing of unmet desires and dreams yet realized.

"The secret affair," Okami says. "Your second child is his. The resemblance is uncanny, but your husband does not notice it."

"We had a child together? Does he know?"

"Of course," Okami says. "His own wife is barren. Their marriage loveless. It was the emptiness in both your lives that drew the two of you together."

"In your next life," Dag says. "You will be together to learn that passion alone cannot sustain a marriage. Nor can convenience. It takes two equals bound together by a destiny greater than themselves to sustain a union."

The Little Light remembers her Ketu in Libra. Venus had blessed her with many suitors, but none of them quite filled the longing in her heart to live out her true destiny.

The Little Light's three former children walk into the room. They kneel on the floor and touch their heads to the ground.

"Your eldest son," Dag says, "will be your father in your next life. And your daughter, born of your great love, will be your mother. And the youngest child will be your brother. For what you have given them in this life, they will have to repay.

"Although you did your duty for them as was expected of you, you gave yourself up in the process. In your next life, you will fulfil your unspoken desire to leave them and live your own life.

"You will spend the first 31 years of your life repaying your karmic debts. Once that is cleared, life will begin preparing you for your new destiny, as the Mother Guardian of the Lore."

The Little Light's three children carry the casket out to the crematorium. There are many people gathered there. The mood is somber and mournful. The cries of all those gathered fills her soul with an incredible heaviness.

One by one, members of her family get on stage to give a eulogy in her honor, describing in detail what a great mother and wife she was. They fight through tears to remain composed and speak through muffled sobs. Other family members gather to give strength when someone cannot go on.

The Little Light remembers her old life – a vague flashback of distant memories that are incoherent and incomprehensible. The fleeting nature of her last human incarnation is like droplets of water all crashing into one and another; there for a moment before it morphs into something else. In the funeral customs of the culture she was born into, it is forbidden to say the name of the deceased once they have passed on, for names can cause the soul to remember.

The Little Light is unable to comprehend why everyone is crying, for death releases one from life and returns the soul to the Great Light. The Little Light realizes that it is our attachments that cause us grief, for life must go on in the cyclical dance of life and death.

"The Great Light was right to choose you," Dag says. "I have done this many times and have never seen a soul so at peace with its passing."

The Little Light's three children carry the body to the funeral pyre. Her eldest son sets the body on fire. The Little Light watches as her old body burns in flames.

The Little Light looks over at Okami, who is slowly fading.

"Mistress," Okami says, "it was my privilege to have served you."

Okami vanishes. Dag and the Little Light watch the body as it turns to ash. Members of her old family cry inconsolably, their sobs intolerable, their suffering unendurable.

At the end of the ceremony, all that's left is ash. So many memories, so many life experiences – all reduced to ash. The family transfers the contents to an urn that looks exactly like the one that Mercury opened in the Cosmic Womb.

"With death," Dag says, "there is always rebirth. Are you ready, Little Light?"

"I am."

"Havah…" Dag whispers. "Havah… It is time."

Chapter 12:

Life is Too Short

When the Little Light opens her eyes, all she sees is bright white light. She blinks over and over again. A blurry scene slowly unfolds in front of her. She is at a hospital. Doctors and nurses surround a pregnant woman who is unconscious. She lies on a bed surrounded by machines. Music plays softly in the background as doctors yell out instructions at the nurses who rush to obey their command. An ethereal blue cord stretches from the woman's womb to the Little Light's belly button.

"Mama," the Little Light says.

"Indeed," Havah says.

The Little Light looks over at Havah, who is wearing a simple white flowing dress.

"She was my daughter in my previous incarnation," the Little Light says.

"I am aware. She was a gifted seer in her last life, and in this life, too. Women take after their fathers. She will be passing on this gift to you."

"I will be a seer?"

"In a sense… It is an unwise to ask so many questions about the future, Liora. The future is not yours to see."

The Little Light nods and returns her gaze to her mother. She remembers the third man she met at her funeral. Some souls are tied together for lifetimes.

"Why is she unconscious?" the Little Light asks.

"It is a caesarean birth," Havah says. "When you denied Venus' gifts, it delayed your time of birth. So, you are overdue…in human time. But in Cosmic Time, everything is as it should be."

The Little Light looks at her mother – the woman whose womb her body grew in for nine months. It is an arduous journey, for mother and baby alike. The Little Light thinks about how she carried this same soul in her womb in her last life.

"I've seen this so many times," Havah says, "and it's a miracle each time. Creation at its most beautiful."

"I was a mother in my last life," the Little Light says. "Will I be one in this life too?"

"Perhaps… Life is not meant to be foretold, Little Light. It is meant to be lived."

The Little Light returns her gaze to her future mother. The doctor makes a cut across the abdomen and womb. Blood trickles out as the doctor tears through tissue to reveal the crown of the baby's head. The process is diffi-cult to watch. *I can't believe I willingly put myself through this three times in my last life.* As the Little Light averts her eyes, she notices an image of a lion engraved on the underside of her mother's right wrist.

"What's that?" the Little Light asks, trying to avoid watching the scene in front of her.

"Her Father Clan totem," Havah says. "The lion is the spirit animal of her paternal ancestors."

"And what's that on her left wrist?"

Havah eyes linger over the image of an azure-colored river with a white swan swimming on top.

"The Motherland totem," Havah says. "It is where your maternal ancestors come from. They are from the Saraswati River."

"Why these totems?" the Little Light asks. "I don't re-member seeing them at my funeral."

"A lot has changed since you died, Little Light. The world has become a messy and complicated place. These totems are a way for humans to identify their origins."

"Our origins? I thought we all emerged from the Great Light."

"It is not that simple anymore."

The baby's head emerges from the womb. The Little Light begins to feel uneasy. *Is that me? I am so small and so helpless. How can that little human grow up to be the future Mother Guardian of the Lore?*

Pirouzeh appears and flies noiselessly through the room. She perches herself on the Little Light's shoulder.

"Welcome to planet earth," Pirouzeh says.

"Thank you, wise one," the Little Light says, still fraught and weak.

Havah leans forward and embraces the Little Light.

"It is time, Liora," Havah says, her voice cracking with emotion, tears in her eyes. "One day, you will be standing where I am. Doing the same for other souls that are born into this world."

The Little Light nods, releasing Havah, feeling more frail with each moment.

"Go forth, my child," Havah says.

The Little Light takes a deep breath. She feels nauseous and fidgety. Pirouzeh flies soundlessly across the room and sinks her beak into the ethereal blue cord that ties the Little Light to her mother. The body the Little Light received in the Cosmic Womb dissipates. It bursts into a million little crystals, showering the room in a fantastic display of bright light.

The Little Light morphs into a candle flame again, as small as a fingernail. The doctors pull the head till the body emerges from the womb. Within moments, the baby cries. No matter how willing the soul, it is a moment of great anguish to be separated from the Great Light and to manifest in human form. The umbilical cord that ties mother to child is cut.

"It's a girl," the doctor says. "Gemini Rising, Sun in Pisces, Moon in Aries with a Pisces midheaven."

"Any birthmark?" the nurse asks.

"A candle flame on her neck. It is Saturn's mark."

"Saturn… Not an easy destiny."

"No great destiny ever is."

Havah smiles as she looks at the tiny baby – the tiny baby whose destiny has been foretold for many millennia. So many incarnations, so many dreams, so many desires, all embedded in a Little Light.

"Maya," Pirouzeh whispers gently. "Your time has come."

Acknowledgments

I would sincerely like to thank my great-grandfather Mancharram Nagindas and my grandfather Ratilal Mancharram. You are no longer in this world – but everything that you have given me and all that you have taught me lives on in me. Thank you, truly. I would not be the person I am today without your guidance and blessings.

I am deeply grateful to my mother, Manjula Kachiwala. She was my very first teacher and after all these years her teachings still continue to light my path and guide my way. I would like to thank my childhood companion and sister Rita Ratilal for her advice. She is one of the most brilliant and intelligent people I know.

My best friend Shubhpreet Kaur has been my strength. We've weathered many storms together as we watched the sun rise on the horizon. I am indebted to my *sensei* Kumi Ohkawara. I will never forget her unwavering devotion and dedication to me during my Japan years.

I would also like to thank: Yougesh Khatri, Guillaume de Lestrange, Fiona Jacob, Swetha Raj, Tal Hurwitz, Vandana Rajendran, Virginie Combet, and Issa Aweel. You have all played a big part towards the realization of my dream of becoming an author.

On the professional front, I would like to thank all the freelancers I have had the pleasure to work with through Fiverr and Reedsy. My manuscript would never have come together without your input. I would like to thank Kristen Abram, Rob Diprose, Megan Szep and Stu Mentha for their feedback and encouragement with the first draft of my manuscript. I am truly fortunate my editor Amanda Nicole Ryan came into my life. She nurtured me as a writer and brought my manuscript to the next level. I would like to thank Aia Naiya Illustration for designing the artwork for the cover and Muhammed Amir for designing the typography.

Lastly, I would like to mention Shannon Donnelly and Mitul Patel for believing in this project and for their work in developing a marketing strategy so that this book could reach its intended audience.

Thank you all so much.

About the Author

Dipa Sanatani is the Merchant of Stories. She comes from a family of merchants and educators with roots in Singapore and the UK. Twelve years ago, she left behind her roots to discover her wings. Since then, she's lived, studied and worked in Australia, Israel, Japan and China, adding uncharted territories to a long list of previously ventured destinations. With a background in both business and education, Dipa has extensive experience in the public-school system as well as in the private, government and corporate sectors.

"No matter where I go, I meet people with the same hopes, the same fears and the same needs for joy, companionship, and adventure. The human experience is a universal one. The things we have in common vastly outweigh that which differentiates us. Our life and time is precious. We must savour it. It is this philosophy I weave through my stories, no matter where the next step of my journey will bring me."

In her debut novel THE LITTLE LIGHT, Dipa explores spiritual and metaphysical themes inspired by world mythology, folklore, fairy tales, and ancient legends; as well as contemporary fiction and YA literature. Through her stories, she tackles the big themes of life, love, and our place in this vast universe, discovering and re-discovering the journey that is life with a deep sense of curiosity and a restless thirst for the next great adventure.

www.dipasanatani.com

Instagram: @mithbook

www.facebook.com/mythbooks

CPSIA information can be obtained
at www.ICGtesting.com
Printed in the USA
FSHW012002070121
77499FS